‘Trust you[illegible]y.’

Marcus heard a small gasp of sound; as he reached up to lift her down, she held herself just beyond the reach of his arms. He could sense a very real agitation.

‘Oh, no, sir! I c-couldn’t! You c-cannot possibly wish to...to...’

She had misunderstood him. He said drily, ‘You are quite right, my dear—I do not wish to! Indeed, I can readily promise you will be quite safe from any attentions of *that* nature.’ She showed no immmediate signs of being reassured. ‘Come!’ he urged. ‘I will solemnly engage *not* to offer for you if nothing less will serve to convince you.’

Sheila Walsh lives in Southport. Her first Regency novel, THE GOLDEN SONGBIRD, won her an award presented by the Romantic Novelists' Association in 1974. She has since written a number of Regency romances, and has twice been shortlisted for the Romantic Novelists' Association Boots Award. A HIGHLY RESPECTABLE MARRIAGE, published as a longer Masquerade, won the 1984 RNA Award for the Best Romantic Novel of the Year.

Previous titles

A WOMAN OF LITTLE IMPORTANCE
THE NABOB
MINERVA'S MARQUIS

THE PINK PARASOL

Sheila Walsh

First published in Great Britain 1991
by Mills & Boon Limited

This edition 1991

ISBN 0 263 77457 0

Masquerade is a trademark published by
Mills & Boon Limited, Eton House,
18–24 Paradise Road, Richmond, Surrey, TW9 1SR.

Set in Times Roman 11¼ on 12 pt.
04-9111-59771 C

Made and printed in Great Britain

CHAPTER ONE

LADY WIGMORE'S missive was, like the lady herself, unambiguous, leaving its recipient in very little doubt of what was expected of him. It was, therefore, no mere accident of fate that the handsome jade timepiece fashioned in the guise of a lion's head which graced the mantel-shelf in the Chinese drawing-room was chiming the hour just as Bunting, her ladyship's butler, admitted Mr Anstruther.

'You are punctual, Marcus. Good. I like punctuality in a man.'

The disembodied voice of Lady Wigmore boomed forth from the depths of a shabby, capacious armchair placed comfortably before the fire, its back set resolutely against the otherwise exquisite room as though rejecting in advance the least hint of criticism of its right to be there.

A gleam of genuine amusement flickered momentarily in the eyes of the rather languid young man who crossed the sumptuous carpet—a much prized souvenir of the third viscount's first expedition to China. Upon reaching his aunt's side he made her an elegant leg, expressed the hope that he found her well, and murmured the usual assurances that he was hers to command.

His politenesses were dismissed with a derisive sniff and he was admonished to, 'Sit down, boy! Sit down. That's if you *can* sit in those deucedly tight drawers!'

'Nothing simpler, ma'am,' murmured her nephew in amiable defence of his biscuit-coloured pantaloons. 'They are fashioned of knit cloth, d'you see?'

'Knit, is it? They'd have been considered indecent in *my* day!' came the unequivocal retort. 'Well, what are you waiting for? Can't abide folk who hover! Sit there, where I can see you.' She flapped an impatient hand in the direction of a flimsy-looking bamboo-backed sofa.

Mr Anstruther complied, disposing himself with ease, secure in the knowledge that the sofa was more comfortable and substantial than it appeared. As always he found himself reflecting that his aunt's chair, squatting incongruously amid so many priceless treasures like an ancient crow in a linnet's cage, was no more at odds with its surroundings than its present incumbent.

Lady Wigmore was impressive. As a young woman her proportions had been Junoesque; now, at seventy, she was awesomely huge. By sheer weight alone she could usually browbeat lesser mortals into doing her bidding, as the members of her household could no doubt testify. Yet for all that she was well-liked, not least by this nephew of hers who, even as a child, had never been cowed by her overwhelming personality. It was this, perhaps, allied to the fact that she had never had children of her own, which accounted for the bond of affection which undoubtedly existed between them.

Her partiality did not however extend to his boutonnière, a glorious confection which she was now viewing with acute disfavour. Mr Anstruther bore her displeasure with fortitude, a glimmer of amusement still lingering in the deceptively lazy green eyes as he fingered his lapel lovingly.

'Do you not care for it, Aunt Constance?'

'No, Marcus, I do not. Makes you look like a damned cicisbeo! Pink roses. Faugh! Why d'you do it, boy?'

It was a fair question. In every other respect Mr Anstruther's appearance could scarce be faulted. His golden-brown hair was arranged in the very latest mode, his coat of blue superfine—supplying proof if proof were needed of Weston's consummate skill—was moulded to his slim figure like a second skin to display a good pair of shoulders, while the dove-grey waistcoat beneath was the very model of discretion. His collar points were not too high, his cravat was complex, yet neat. In fact, Mr Anstruther looked exactly what he was—a most notable Corinthian.

Still smiling faintly, he sighed. 'Why, my dear? I thought the whole world knew why. I am fallen hopelessly in love with Rosanne Devine and have sworn to wear pink roses until she consents to return my regard. My man rides up each morning with fresh ones from my hothouses at Holmbury.'

'Humbug! Sheer humbug!' Lady Wigmore fixed him with a fierce glare. 'Y're a poseur, sir! I trust you don't think to bamboozle me with such flim-flam?'

'Certainly not, dear Aunt. You are by far too acute.' He crossed one leg over the other, displaying in so doing the shapely calf which was a constant source of gratification to his valet. His eyes took on a faintly malicious twinkle. 'But it would astonish you to learn how much speculative interest my poor roses evoked at Sally Jersey's soirée last evening!'

'It wouldn't, y'know!' There was a curious rumbling in the vastness of his aunt's bosom which he took to signify mirth. 'I am well aware that there are fools aplenty among Lady Jersey's set ready and willing to swallow your fictions, but they don't know you as I do!'

That was true, he mused, considering how much of his youth had been spent in this house. Lulled by his surroundings into happy reminiscence, he recalled how he had once presumed to quiz his aunt upon her marked partiality for the room in which they now sat, which to his then-untutored way of thinking sat so ill with her robust personality. Rather to his surprise, having damned his impudence, she had admitted in a brusque, almost offhand fashion that she found its atmosphere spiritually uplifting. To the fifteen-year-old boy he had been it seemed such a rum explanation that he'd assumed—though he'd sense enough even then not to say so—that she was cutting him a fine old wheedle. But now, seeing the room at its best, bathed in pale winter sunshine, he was able to appreciate exactly what she had meant.

The Wigmores' Chinese room had caused something of a sensation when, rather more than a hundred years before, the present viscount's father had returned from his first visit to the Orient imbued with a deep and abiding passion for everything Chinese—quite extraordinary in a hitherto undemonstrative man. He came laden with the treasures that were to form the nucleus of this present collection; the wallpaper, which still adorned the walls as fresh as the day it was hung, depicted with exquisite delicacy the strange exotic world whence it came. For the only time in his life the third viscount had enjoyed brief notoriety as one of the prime instigators of a fashion that was to sweep the country, giving rise to a positive plethora of chinoiserie—a fashion that the Prince Regent had recently revived in his pavilion at Brighton. Yet few, if any, of Lord Wigmore's copyists had succeeded in capturing the essential simplicity of the original, reflected Mr Anstruther.

'How is my uncle?' The fourth viscount having inherited his father's passion for exploration, Mr

Anstruther had met his uncle but briefly over the years. He nevertheless enquired after him as always with dutiful concern.

'Oh, you know Wigmore!' said his spouse with cheerful unconcern. 'When last I heard, he was mounting an expedition to some benighted and hitherto uncharted wilderness. But he ain't much of a hand at letter-writing.' Her lord thus satisfactorily disposed of, she turned to more pressing matters. 'But I didn't invite you here in order to make polite conversation, nor to be treated to an account of your doings. Fact is, Marcus—I'm in need of your help.'

It was perhaps fortunate that Bunting chose this precise moment to enter, bearing a tray. Lady Wigmore's commissions had an uncanny knack of disrupting the even tenor of one's life and thereby involving one in the most acute discomfort. The disposal of the tray and the pouring of the Madeira afforded Mr Anstruther time in which to collect his thoughts. The ritual accomplished, he felt able to face his aunt, glass in hand, with every assumption of interest.

'I'm to have my godchild staying with me during the coming Season,' said her ladyship, impatient of the interruption.

'Wasn't aware that you had one, ma'am,' said her nephew, warily unhelpful.

'Well, I have. She's Cecily Merton . . . Camden's gel.'

'Lord Camden?' Mr Anstruther lifted an expressive eyebrow. 'I suppose you know he's running with some very loose fish these days? His name is fast becoming a byword at every gambling hell in town. I did hear that he was discreetly advised to steer clear of White's for the present.' He regarded the glowing liquid in his glass with deceptive casualness. 'Could make things a trifle awkward, wouldn't you say?'

'Of course it will be awkward... devilish awkward, drat the man! Bad enough having him here at all. Bound to set tongues clacking. Bringing the child out is his responsibility, after all, as I didn't scruple to tell him. Sent for him last week—told him... living in rooms when there's that great house in Grosvenor Square standing empty...'

'I bet he loved you for your frankness,' drawled Mr Anstruther. 'Shouldn't think he can afford to open that place up, let alone accomplish his daughter's debut.'

'So he informed me, without so much as a blush! Just treated me to that infernally charming smile of his and declared that he could hardly be expected to carry the affair off satisfactorily without the support of his wife and that the child would in any case do much better with me. Incorrigible rogue! He knew well enough that I'd already half-promised Lady Camden...' She met her nephew's look with a certain wryness. 'Ah, well—Elinor's a poor sort of creature... always ailing, y'know... though what with Camden's profligate ways and a brood of young Mertons—all gels—to rear with little real expectation of establishing them half-way creditably, not to mention her only son, killed at Vittoria, I doubt she's had much joy of her life!' Lady Wigmore sniffed. 'Suspected how it would be, mind, the day I stood godmother to young Cecily. Incredible that the child is now eighteen. Should've kept in touch more, I suppose, but they never came to town, and you know I'm not much of a one for travelling...' Guilt was very much in evidence as she added, 'Still time to make up for that a bit now, eh?'

Mr Anstruther was filled with deep foreboding. 'Do you think that quite wise, Aunt Constance? If you'll be guided by me, you'd much better not get involved.'

'I ain't interested in your opinions, lad.' Lady Wigmore's chins quivered with indignation. 'Mercy on us, I had not thought you were grown so cynical and uncaring!' Another baleful glance directed at his boutonnière spoke volumes. 'Of course I must do what I can for young Cecily! My only hope is that she'll take.' She sighed, and became brisk again. 'No use being mealymouthed about it, Marcus—the child must marry money, and quickly. And that, my boy, is where you come in.'

Mr Anstruther choked on his Madeira and turned pale. 'You don't want me to offer for her?'

Lady Wigmore chuckled; to his oversensitive ears it was a fiendish sound. 'If I thought there was the least possibility of your attending me, I might make a push to secure your interest; Lord knows, you've been the ripest plum on the marriage mart these years past! But I hope I know better than to waste time pursuing vain causes!'

He set his glass down on the little japanned table at his elbow, relief finding expression in a fleeting grin. '*Jeunes filles* have never been my style, you see,' he pleaded in mitigation.

'So I am led to believe!' Her ladyship's voice was dry. And then, as if overcome by curiosity, 'D'you care for no one, Marcus?'

There was a moment of silence. 'I am, I trust, a dutiful and affectionate son to my parents,' he said politely. 'And I am prodigiously fond of you, dear Aunt, as you must be aware...'

'Don't be obtuse with me, boy! You know well enough what I mean.'

'Yes.' He sighed. 'But I was rather hoping to avoid an inquisition.'

'Which is a polite way of telling me to mind my own business, eh?'

His eyes kindled. 'I hope I shall not be obliged to put it so crudely, Aunt Constance. The fact is, I have but recently survived a prolonged and emotionally charged interview with Mama upon a similar theme. She longs to see me married with a brood of little Anstruthers about my feet.' A faint, but unmistakable shudder ran through him. 'As if my sister's three were not enough to satisfy her!'

'Good Lord! Has Hester three, now? Still, you will *have* to marry one day. Your father won't live forever, y'know. And you don't want to end up like Wigmore—with some obscure little pip-squeak for heir.' Casually she added, 'Should've thought there were any number of eligible females eager to pick up the handkerchief an' you dropped it?'

'There are,' he said—and there was an unfamiliar hardness in his voice that warned her to proceed no further.

'Anyhow,' she said, 'I ain't asking you to court Cecily! Just to single her out a little... give us your escort to a function or two... Almack's, that sort of thing. You'll know the way of it.' Again the chuckle. 'They tell me your approbation carries as much weight as George Brummell's these days!' And when he made no immediate reply, but sat smoothing the sofa's bamboo frame absent-mindedly with a well-shaped thumb, 'Lord, Marcus—it's not a lot to ask of you and it could make all the difference in the world to that poor girl's chances. Oh, and should you chance to number among your circle of acquaintances some young man of wealth and breeding who's hanging out for a wife, I'd be vastly obliged if you would steer him in Cecily's direction. After all, whatever may be her short-comings, one cannot quarrel with her breeding, and if she's taken after her mama, which seems very likely, for girls most often do, she will make the most amenable of wives!'

And if she had taken after her papa? As a supposition it seemed equally likely to Mr Anstruther's way of thinking, but he did not venture to air his thoughts, having no wish to prolong further a topic which was fast becoming tedious. He therefore agreed, amid the vaguest pleasantries he could muster with sincerity, that Aunt Constance had but to let him know when Lady Cecily arrived and he would do the necessary. He did not voice a further profound aspiration that the girl would not prove to be too boring, gauche, and provincial, for he could feel no real conviction of its being realised. Instead, as was his invariable practice when faced with anything of a disagreeable nature, he promptly put the matter from his mind.

Several weeks later, he returned from a pleasant and profitable visit to Newmarket to find a blistering note from Aunt Constance awaiting him. The time had come to redeem his rash promise; indeed, he had already been looked for in vain, it seemed. If, his aunt's missive had concluded in her most trenchant tones, he could spare a few moments from his pressing round of engagements, she would very much appreciate his attendance at the small introductory soirée she was to give for Lady Cecily Merton that very evening. His plans had been very much otherwise, for he had been curious to discover to what extent his absence had affected

Rosanne Devine. If he had not mistaken the matter, she had been much put out by his unexpected departure for Newmarket. A promise was a promise, however, and an hour's stay at his aunt's should more than suffice to set his mark of approval upon the unknown godchild.

But from one cause and another it was late when Mr Anstruther arrived in Portland Place, and to his surprise he was obliged to leave his carriage some distance away and walk through a crush of vehicles to his destination. In the lofty vestibule he surrendered his high-crowned hat and his gold crutch cane to one waiting footman and his cloak to another, before making his way down the half-dozen steps leading to the tessellated marble hall, banked upon all sides for the occasion with a profusion of fragrant spring flowers set among potted palms.

Here he was met by Bunting, who greeted him with a shade more of enthusiasm than he was wont to permit himself.

'A *small* soirée, Bunting?' observed Mr Anstruther, one eyebrow lifting imperceptibly.

'It is most gratifying, sir. The number of acceptances was much greater than her ladyship had anticipated—the Season not being fully underway as yet.' The butler gave a discreet little cough. 'May I be permitted to say, sir, that her ladyship will be *very* happy to know that you are come. We have been looking for you these several days past.'

Not by so much as a flicker did Bunting betray that the young gentleman had been found wanting, but from long acquaintance Mr Anstruther was familiar with every nuance of the old butler's fruity tones.

'In disgrace, am I?' His lazy grin was unabashed. 'Ah, well...' He declined Bunting's suggestion that he should perhaps announce him, the formal reception being at an end, lifted a dismissive hand and strolled towards the imposing staircase curving away out of view, whence floated the indistinct strains of a melody struggling valiantly for supremacy against an unremitting tide of laughter and conversation.

He had scarcely taken more than a few steps, however, when a slight figure came hurtling down upon him. With an agility quite astonishing in a gentleman of such apparent indolence he caught and steadied the fleeing girl.

'Oh!' She clutched ineffectually at the revers of his plain black swallow-tailed coat and blinked rapidly several times to clear a film of angry tears from wide-set eyes that were of a soft grey with just a hint of violet in their depths. She was young; no more than eighteen, he judged—the too-thin pointed face had good bones, the line of her jaw delicately defined, a small straight nose. One day, he thought, she could well be a beauty. But now her pale hair, though it shone like silk, was drawn too severely into a high knot and the result, unrelieved by any softening fall of curls, gave her an added look of brittle vulnerability. She wore that obligatory uniform of a *jeune fille*—the little white dress.

'F-forgive me, sir! I wasn't looking...' The words trailed off. She was plainly distressed; her voice, pleasingly light, was choked with the force of her emotions.

Mr Anstruther rescued his mutilated lapels from her grasp and set her gently but firmly back on her feet, smiled with an engaging, apologetic whimsicality, and bade her think no more about it. His words, however, seemed only to provoke fresh agitation.

'Oh, I'm s-so sorry!' she cried. 'Your beautiful coat!' Her fingers flew out again instinctively to smooth it, but this time he was quick to intercept the gesture.

'My dear young lady, I beg you will not distress yourself any further! It is but a trifling garment—a crease or two will scarce be noticed.' His glance became more acute. 'Is there perhaps some way in which I may serve you?'

She seemed to shrink a little at his words. 'Oh, no!' A nervous hand flew to her throat. 'I... thank you, but...No!' She was gone without another word, running down the remaining stairs towards the conservatory in a flurry of gauze.

Mr Anstruther lingered for a moment staring after her, his expression pensive. With one hand indecisively on the banister, he looked for Bunting, but the butler had discreetly effaced himself. He shrugged and resumed his leisurely progress.

Upstairs, he found both drawing-rooms impressively filled. His aunt had done well, he mused, counting at least three of the town's most influential hostesses, lured there, he suspected, as much by curiosity as any more charitable motive. The presence of the Baroness von Oppenheimer alone was more than sufficient to establish the interest of others. It pleased him to note that though Lady Wigmore moved little in fashionable circles she was yet able to command a formidable acquaintance.

Putting up his glass and appearing oblivious of the stir his arrival had created, he allowed his eye to rove at will. In the front drawing-room he noted Emily Cowper seated upon a sofa, and with her, the amiable Lady Sefton—both shrewdly selected, he had little doubt, with a view to obtaining vouchers for Almack's.

In the Chinese room a lively group of young people occupied the centre of the floor. The preponderance of excitable females among the group was readily explained by the figure rising out of their midst—a well-shaped head of tumbling black hair and a set of handsome military side-whiskers set off by the unmistakable magnificence of a red coat embellished with gilded epaulettes. The young officer, upon seeing Mr Anstruther, lifted a hand in cheerful greeting; in a moment the group parted reluctantly to allow him through and he strode across the room, his ebony cane ostentatiously supporting a pronounced limp.

'Playing the brave wounded hero, I see, Harry,' drawled Mr Anstruther, but there was so much warmth in his eyes as to rob the words of any malice. The greeting was received by Major Harry Ireland with an appreciative chuckle as the two clasped hands.

'Coming from anyone but you, dear boy, I would diagnose an outsize bout of jealousy.' The crinkles at the corners of his eyes deepened. 'But with your address it cannot be so! D'you know, Marcus, I had no idea a ball through the leg could add so considerably to one's consequence. It quite resigns one to the attendant inconveniences.'

'Does the wound pain you very much?' said Mr Anstruther in a very different voice as he saw at close quarters the lines of strain which no amount of banter could disguise.

His friend gave a wry grimace. 'No more than one can reasonably contain. And at all events, I count myself fortunate that I still have my leg when so many have lost their lives.' A momentary blank-eyed intensity gave way to a self-conscious laugh. 'Oh, God, Marcus! Don't encourage me to grow maudlin, not here, of all places!' And then, with deliberate lightness, 'You know, Lady Wigmore's gunning for you? I gather you're late, my lad—

about four days late, to be precise. I hope you've a good excuse!'

'Oh, I'll turn the old girl up sweet, never fear!' Mr Anstruther dismissed his impending fate in favour of a more pressing matter. 'Harry—I've just had the most intriguing encounter with a girl...'

'I might have known it was something in the petticoat line! Prime little article, was she?' said Major Ireland with a knowing grin. 'Well, I shouldn't tell *that* to Lady W. You'll need to dream up a much worthier tale to excuse your tardiness...'

'Be silent, addlepate,' commanded Mr Anstruther amiably, 'and listen, if you will. The girl was here, but a moment since—pale little thing—particularly fine eyes—but all arms and legs like an untrained colt...' he mused, remembering. 'Tendency to stammer.'

'Looked as though a breath of wind'd snap her in two?'

'That's her.'

'Sounds like Lady Cecily Merton, Lady Wigmore's protégée.'

'Ah!' murmured Mr Anstruther with no great degree of surprise.

'I'd hazard it ain't been the happiest of debuts for the child. Pity you weren't here from the start. I suspect she heard something she wasn't meant to...one or two of the old cats have had their claws out. Baroness von Oppenheimer was particularly outspoken, I believe...you know how she can be!

Thing is, Camden arrived a trifle bosky and brought with him some deuced cit he goes around with these days—name of Elliston. D'you know him?—a regular Captain Sharp if I ever saw one—and, what with him ogling Lady Cecily fit to put her to the blush and Camden doing nothing to cast a damper in his way, your aunt's in a fair miff.'

'Marcus!' As though summoned by Harry's words, the crowds parted and the majestic figure of Lady Wigmore bore down upon Mr Anstruther like an avenging colossus enveloped in purple crêpe, her head wreathed in a turban, her chins wobbling ominously above a heavy collar studded with diamonds and rubies which seemed to be embedded in her plump neck. She prodded him painfully with her fan, then shook it open to cool her flushed face.

'Where have you been, wretched boy? Just when I most had need of you!'

'My deepest apologies, Aunt Constance—I was unavoidably detained.' He lifted her heavily be-ringed hand reverently to his lips. 'I expect you have already been told that you are looking particularly well this evening.'

'No, I have not!' she retorted, though there was a half-appreciative twinkle in her eye. 'Nor, as you well know, do I deal in Spanish coin, so it's no use wasting one of your pretty speeches on me. Really, Marcus, it is a great deal too bad of you when I had *such* hopes!'

'Oh, come, ma'am—that's doing it a bit too brown,' drawled Mr Anstruther, allowing his glance to stray around the room. 'Seems a very agreeable gathering—impressive, even, so early in the Season—wouldn't you say so, Harry? With one or two exceptions, that is.' His eye had lighted upon a gentleman who had dressed with such obvious care as to make the result of his efforts doubly unfortunate. Camden's friend! He shuddered imperceptibly. 'I had not supposed Jack Elliston to be on your visiting list, Aunt?'

'He is not!' Lady Wigmore's vast bosom heaved with indignation. 'But I could hardly show the creature the door when Cecily's own father brought him. Had to stand there and receive him and look pleasant about it—quite the most mortifying experience I have been obliged to endure in many a long day—and as for poor Cecily...' She turned abruptly to Major Ireland. 'Harry, where is the child? Have you seen her? I left her in the care of Mrs Longford.'

Harry Ireland, who looked as though he would more willingly have faced a troop of French cavalry, cast a nervous glance at Mr Anstruther, smoothed his fine whiskers, and cleared his throat. 'Fact is, ma'am, Lady Cecily left the room rather hurriedly...seemed a little *distraite*...believe she might have overheard a certain indiscreet remark...'

'Don't say another word!' boomed Lady Wigmore. 'It was Tilly von Oppenheimer, was it not? Lord, that woman's tongue has the sting of the devil at times. For my own part, I vow I wouldn't have her under my roof, but in the circumstances—well, they tell me her assemblies are quite exclusive, so I deemed it politic to swallow my pride. But she'd best have a care! She'll queer my gel's chances at her peril.'

Mr Anstruther exchanged a speaking glance with his friend; instinctively all three turned simultaneously to focus attention upon a mature, graceful vision in pale lace trimmed with pink swansdown who was holding court near the door. One curling pink ostrich plume secured by a diamond pin complimented a coiffure that bore glowing testament to her hairdresser's consummate skill.

'It's hennaed, of course!' Lady Wigmore's voice sank to an acerbic whisper. 'Paints her face, too, y'know.'

As though conscious of their interest, the Baroness von Oppenheimer looked across the room and graciously inclined her head.

Mr Anstruther, who had faced the prospect of an unconscionably dull evening in the most grudging of humours, was beginning to enjoy himself hugely. 'Shall I stare her out of countenance, dear Aunt?' he offered helpfully.

She gave a sudden crack of laughter. 'Lord, I'd give a monkey to see her face, an' you did! But I believe I needn't put you to the trouble, m'boy. I can bring Tilly von Oppenheimer to heel any time

I choose!' Lady Wigmore, returning the baroness's civility with equal punctiliousness and urging her companions to do likewise, was suddenly, fiendishly, confident. 'One of the few people left, d'ye see, who remembers when she was plain Matilda Waters with nothing to recommend her but her looks.' She uttered an unladylike snort. 'Landed the baron in his dotage and led the poor man a rare old dance! He was dead within a twelvemonth—in fact, shortly after she was delivered of that milksop son we all charitably acknowledge to be his...'

Intrigued, her audience demanded further enlightenment, and Lady Wigmore, nothing loath, obliged. It was never clear, she confided, whether the baron knew how ruthlessly he was being cuckolded but one way or another it didn't stop him leaving his relict sufficiently well-endowed to indulge every whim a beautiful, silly woman could fall prey to.

'Which,' said Lady Wigmore complacently, 'she has done quite predictably, ever since. But as the boy grew, his origins became increasingly obvious to anyone who remembered Willie von Oppenheimer as a young man—*that* creature of passionate charm and wit could never have sired such a pudding-faced mamby-pamby. So you see,' she concluded with a certain ghoulish satisfaction, 'I have only to mention 'the old days' to make Tilly turn as green as an overhung pheasant under all that rouge!'

Major Ireland chuckled aloud while Mr Anstruther said, with a severity belied by the awed gleam in his eyes, 'Aunt Constance—you are utterly shameless!'

'I know. But I've grown mightily fond of that child in these past few days and I'll not have her slighted.' She heaved a mighty sigh. 'Unfortunately, it wouldn't advance Cecily's cause one jot to make an enemy of Tilly, so I'll remain civil, though it turns my bile to do so. Now I suppose I must find that silly child and persuade her to return. She don't want for spirit, mind, but I wouldn't blame her if she'd sought refuge in her room and declined to leave it again tonight.'

'I'll wager she hasn't done so,' said Mr Anstruther with so much assurance that she stared.

'But you ain't even acquainted with Cecy!'

'No,' he agreed with a slight smile. 'We have not precisely been introduced—but I believe I know where she may be.'

CHAPTER TWO

THE conservatory door gave a protesting creak as Mr Anstruther pushed it open and stepped inside. He stood for a moment among the giant ferns, allowing his eyes time to adjust. In the warm humid darkness the earthy tang of the greenery was sharp in his nostrils as it mingled with other, subtler perfumes. A high domed glass roof gleamed translucently under a full moon which sheened the plants, turning the drooping fronds of fern to delicate silver filigree.

'Lady Cecily?' he called softly.

There was a long silence broken only by the faint splash of water and then, 'Go away!' came the muffled, ungracious retort.

Mr Anstruther accepted the rebuff philosophically and moved in the direction whence it had been delivered, picking his way carefully along meandering pathways and, as these took unexpected turns, silently cursing his aunt's predilection for ornamental pools. As he extricated his feet for the umpteenth time from a near-watery disaster, the sheer folly of what he was about to do was borne in upon him. He hesitated, half inclined to turn back.

And then he saw her.

She was sitting above him on a ledge, her feet tucked up under her after the fashion of a child, chin cupped in hand, staring out on the cool anonymity of the rose garden. The same moonlight which lay like water across the gardens lent her the timeless grace of a Greek statue. She made no move, no sign that she had even noticed his presence.

Mr Anstruther leaned one shoulder against the cold glass of the conservatory window and folded his arms. 'Should you very much mind if I join you?' he asked, and continued without waiting for answer, 'How clever of you to have discovered this place—I had thought that I was the only one who knew of it. I expect, like me, you were finding the gathering upstairs particularly tiresome...so riddled as it is with tattlemongers and pretentious bores. I try to avoid such occasions, but with Lady Wigmore it is sometimes impossible—her invitations do tend to adopt the tone of a royal command to which one cannot but accede.'

'As you were obliged to do this evening?' she said at last in a stifled voice.

'Oh, this evening I had a most particular reason for wishing to come,' he said, choosing his words with care. 'A friend of mine was invited—Harry Ireland—perhaps you know him? He's a casualty of the fight against Boney—sustained his wound, poor devil, when the war was all but over. I had thought to commiserate with him, but find him instead the darling of the ladies and enjoying every minute.'

Her head lifted abruptly as he spoke and, too late, he remembered her brother's fate. It was unlike him to be so clumsy. 'Forgive me,' he said quietly. 'War is not a subject for levity. Let us talk of happier things. I have not seen you before this evening, I think—are you newly come to London?'

She stirred as though impatient of his fictions. 'You need not humour me, sir. I may be an *insignificant, up-from-the-country miss*... b-but I am not stupid! I guessed who you were from the first.' Here a note of bitterness crept in. 'Indeed, you would be amazed to learn how often your name has cropped up in her ladyship's conversation these past few days. She has been at the greatest pains to assure me of the exalted position in society enjoyed by her splendid nephew, the noted nonpareil—how he had but to smile upon me for all the world to follow suit. She has impressed upon me how fortunate I must own myself in being able to count upon your approbation.' Indignation was beginning to choke her words. 'Well, Mr Anstruther—I don't want that kind of approbation... I have n-no wish to fly false colours... and since you have made it quite plain that you don't really care a jot I absolve you here and now from any tiresome undertaking you might have g-given your aunt!'

It was a brave speech. Mr Anstruther wondered if she had any idea how brave—to reject in so cavalier a fashion the patronage of one of the few people in London who could make or break her. Yet the stirring of anger he felt within him was almost wholly directed against his aunt. How *could* she have contrived to bungle matters so badly? Her motives might have been of the best, but she had been deplorably heavy-handed!

He stepped away from the window and came to look up at the girl, his profile clearly etched against the light. 'My dear girl,' he said. 'Do I strike you as the kind of man who would permit himself to be so used?'

He sensed rather than saw the beginnings of uncertainty. 'N-no...' came the reply, and then, with more confidence, 'but I can see exactly how it must have been, for Lady Wigmore can be very persuasive and I know that you and she are very c-close. What more natural than that she should beg you to take pity on her poor little god-child...?' Quite unconsciously, but with devastating accuracy, she mimicked Lady Wigmore's fruity tones. 'She's just eighteen, poor gel...and desperately in need of a husband! No dowry, I fear...the father hasn't a feather to fly with, and with three younger gels at home to be thought of, not to mention an ailing mama, it ain't going to be easy! But with the nonpareil to bring her into fashion...and the name, of course—a Camden is not to be sniffed at—we may well find someone sufficiently plump in the pocket to waive the vexed question of the dowry in order to gain privilege of calling his wife Lady Cecily.'

It was a long speech and she hadn't stammered once. Furthermore, it was so very close to what Lady Wigmore had in fact said to him that he was convinced she must have overheard his aunt talking to one of her cronies. She dropped the false voice and her eyes turned towards him, glittering with unshed tears. 'Someone like Mr Elliston, perhaps?'

'Elliston!' For a moment he was shocked out of his composure. 'Good God! My aunt wouldn't entertain *his* suit, surely?'

There was a sound rather like a strangled sob. 'Perhaps not. But I f-fear my father will. He...they are acquainted, you see, and if he w-wanted it...' Lady Cecily's voice took on a note of defiance. 'I believe Papa owes him money.'

'Very likely,' said Mr Anstruther in a deliberately matter-of-fact way. 'Nothing in the least unusual in that. I should estimate that half London owes Mr Elliston money.'

Lady Cecily scrambled to her feet, dislodging a loose stone, which fell into the pool below with a small splash. There was in her stance the kind of awkward dignity that only the young possessed.

'I am obliged to you, sir, for your tact, but I have long been aware of my father's weakness. The economies that one has been obliged to make with regard to the household accounts are such as must...' Here she stopped as though suddenly conscious that she was betraying family secrets. Her voice shook a little as she continued, 'It is simply that until I c-came to London I had not fully appreciated the extent of Papa's . . . involvement. I can only thank God that Mama doesn't know the whole! Oh, dear—that sounds dreadfully disloyal to Papa and I didn't mean it to be so, for though we don't see him as often as I could wish he is indeed the kindest of fathers—he came home especially, you know, in order that he might himself bring me to London, when I dare say he could quite easily have arranged matters otherwise.'

Mr Anstruther took a jaundiced view of this selfless picture she presented of the earl, but he did not feel it his place to offer opinions upon the duties and responsibilities of a father. Lady Cecily, however, totally misunderstood his somewhat pensive look.

'It was heedless of me, was it not?' she sighed. 'Bella is always accusing me of speaking too impulsively and I c-can see that she is right . . .'

'Bella?'

'My sister, Mr Anstruther. She is fifteen and already much more sensible than I shall ever be.'

There was a touch of wistfulness in this resigned acknowledgement which moved him to reassure her that he had not thought her remarks in the least disloyal or in any way lacking in respect.

'Well, I'm glad, because I hope I am a d-dutiful

daughter, and, though I'm not awfully good at explaining how I feel, I *do know* what is expected of me... the necessity to make an advantageous marriage, and I don't mean to be missish! I d-dare say it might not be so bad if only——' she sighed '—if only it need not be someone like Mr Elliston! There...' The note of truculence crept back. 'I expect now you think me dreadfully selfish?'

'On the contrary, I find your reasoning remarkably sound,' said Mr Anstruther with unimpaired calm. 'To be obliged to contemplate Mr Elliston as a possible husband must offend the sensibilities of any gently nurtured young lady.'

There followed a silence pregnant with suspicion. 'Are you quizzing me, Mr Anstruther?'

'Certainly not,' he drawled. 'I was never more serious. I do, however, feel that you are troubling yourself unnecessarily.'

'Perhaps.' Lady Cecily seemed depressingly unconvinced. 'But suppose Mr Elliston *does* offer for me? We have only met twice, but his attentions were so marked on both occasions—I d-didn't know where to look! And I dare say he must be very wealthy, you know,' she concluded naïvely, 'if he can afford to lend so many people money, so I should think Papa would be bound to favour his suit. Do you not think it likely, sir?'

He thought it more than likely, if Lord Camden was as deep in debt as rumour had him. It was at this point that Mr Anstruther began to suffer unexpected qualms of conscience. He had come this evening prepared to endure the boredom of such a gathering for as long as it took to set his seal of approval upon his aunt's little country mouse. But he had reckoned without the aforesaid mouse, who had somehow succeeded in unsettling him with her ingenuous frankness and the tendency to stammer in moments of stress which he found curiously endearing. He could, of course, stand aside and watch the innocence crushed out of her, as it inevitably must be by the insidious cruelties of this fashionable world in which he lived. He had seen it happen often enough; indeed Lady Cecily had already had a foretaste of Tilly von Oppenheimer's acid tongue. He found the prospect of her eventual mortification almost as distasteful to him as the thought of such innocence married off willy-nilly to that gull-groper Elliston.

'I think it possible,' he said with a barely perceptible shrug of resignation. 'In which case I can see but one alternative, Lady Cecily. You had really much better trust yourself to me.'

He heard a small gasp of sound; as he reached up to lift her down, she held herself just beyond the reach of his arms. He could sense a very real agitation.

'Oh, no, sir! I c-couldn't! You c-cannot possibly wish to...to...'

She had misunderstood him. He said drily, 'You are quite right, my dear—I do not wish to! Indeed, I can readily promise you will be quite safe from any attentions of *that* nature.' She showed no immediate signs of being reassured. 'Come!' he urged. 'I will solemnly engage *not* to offer for you if nothing else will serve to convince you.'

Still she hesitated. He curbed a very natural exasperation, tinged not a little with pique, as he wondered briefly why he was putting himself to so much trouble for a chit who quite obviously did not appreciate the signal honour being accorded to her, and said with an air of quizzical reproach, 'Lady Cecily, I beg you will not oblige me to climb up and fetch you. The merest speck upon my coat, the least suggestion of damp feet, and I must endure the severe displeasure of my valet. If you knew Trimm, I am persuaded you would not be so unkind.'

'Oh, but that is absurd!' she cried, betrayed into a spontaneous trill of laughter.

'Of course! Life is frequently absurd. Do you not find it so? Come now!' he commanded again, and this time she offered no resistance as he swung her down and set her on her feet. She was taller than he remembered, and slender as a wand. Lord! Was there ever anything so young and defenceless? he wondered as her eyes searched his face half shyly. Two hovering tears, blinked free, ran in silver rivulets down her cheeks. He smoothed them away with competent fingers and at once she stepped back, embarrassed, turning away to toy with a nodding frond of fern.

'I have behaved very stupidly,' she said at last in a rather subdued voice; and, when he made no attempt to disagree with her, added with more resolution, 'And I have let down Lady Wigmore when she has been so very good to me.' She swung round as though suddenly having done with meekness. 'Only I was so angry, you s-see——'

'Don't!' He cut her short. 'What is done, is done. Pray strive to resist the very natural inclination to justify your behaviour. Nothing, believe me, is so tedious as self-recrimination.'

He had been unnecessarily curt, but she did not flinch; rather, her head lifted a fraction. Not such a mouse, after all, perhaps!

'Then tell me, sir—how can I best set the matter right?' she asked quietly.

He took her chin between long slim fingers, raising her face to the light. His faint lazy smile conveyed grudging approval. 'Will you place yourself unreservedly in my hands?' A slight movement of her head signified assent. 'Sensible girl. Then, for now you need do very little. We will return to the party and you will strive to look as though you had never been away. I shall get my aunt to take you across to sit with Lady Sefton and Lady Cowper...' Consternation widened her eyes. He tapped her cheek reprovingly and released her. 'Goose! They won't eat you and it will be politic to court their approval. Their approbation——' his mouth quirked '—carries almost as much weight as mine! Comport yourself well and I am prepared to wager that before much above a week is out half of fashionable London will be beating a path to Aunt Constance's door eager to make the acquaintance of Mr Anstruther's latest flirt.'

'Oh, but . . .' She looked less impressed than she ought.

'But what?'

'Well, I shan't be, shall I? Your . . . flirt, I m-mean . . .'

'To the world it will appear so.' Impatience jarred Mr Anstruther's voice slightly. 'Do you doubt my ability to bring it off?'

'Oh, no! I wouldn't presume to d-doubt you, sir. But I cannot think it entirely honest in me to pretend to be what I am not.'

'I see.' He resisted the temptation to tell her that honesty was an indulgence rarely practiced to any purpose in those circles she would be required to frequent. 'And what, pray, are you?'

Lady Cecily considered the question with frowning gravity. 'I'm not sure.' She glanced down at her pretty but unmodish dress, fingering the light gauze thoughtfully. 'A simple country-bred girl without ambition, I suppose . . .' Her eyes met his unexpectedly with something approaching a roguish grin. 'And I have learned enough of the nonpareil to know that *that* is not his style at all!'

Surprised yet again by her quickness and the cheerful resilience of her nature, he chuckled with appreciation. 'So much the better! Only consider how it will intrigue society to see us so often together.'

'You speak as if it were a game, sir?'

'So it is, and a vastly entertaining one at that.' He saw that she was troubled and, on impulse, lifted her hand lightly to his lips, his eyes still amused, but kindly so. 'But it shan't hurt you, my dear child, I promise. Will you trust me?'

'Yes,' she said simply.

Just like that. No more than a moment's hesitation before taking his word. The degree of confidence she apparently placed in him on such brief acquaintance was, to say the least, unnerving. He released her hand and said, a little abruptly, 'Come along, then. If you feel quite ready?'

She hung back. 'Will people not think it odd if we appear together?'

He looked amused. 'My dear child, if we are to deal together, you will have to accustom yourself to believing that no one ever presumes to question what I do!' She uttered a stifled sound that made him look quickly down at her. 'Are you by any chance laughing at me?'

'I just thought...it might be a bit like being God!'

'Impertinent baggage!' But she was right! Though more likely the devil had a hand in it, for of all the quixotic, cross-brained, incomprehensible idiocy...He caught himself half grinning as he took her arm. Egad, but the situation did have a certain piquant allure!

He thought fleetingly of Rosanne—fate seemed determined to throw a rub in their way. He was surprised to find how little he minded. The pursuit of Rosanne had been an amusing diversion, but already—perhaps, because he sensed she was on the point of surrender—the chase had lost a little of its savour. Unobtrusively Mr Anstruther removed the single pink rosebud from his lapel and tossed it, with only the vaguest of regrets, into one of his aunt's ornamental pools, whence it was symbolically borne from his sight on the gently moving water.

Almost the first person they encountered upon reaching the Chinese room was the Earl of Camden. At first glance he presented the image any daughter might take pride in: handsome, debonair—in his dress he was almost the equal of Mr Anstruther—and of a devil-may-care disposition. It took a discerning eye to notice what a daughter could not be expected to look for—a certain falseness in the joviality, the strain behind eyes that were restlessly, brilliantly blue.

'Well, well—there you are, puss! Being well looked after, I see. Splendid...splendid! Your servant, Mr Anstruther.' His restless eyes met faint disparagement in the nonpareil's lazy green gaze and slid away. The earl was undoubtedly badly disguised, but carried it well. A faint cough at his shoulder called him back to his duty. 'And here is poor Jack, just hoping for a sight of you, m'dear...'

Mr Anstruther felt Lady Cecily go tense under his touch.

'D'you know Mr Elliston, Anstruther? Deuced good friend of mine.'

The words seemed to come out with an effort. Mr Anstruther bowed coldly and the young man at Lord Camden's side returned the bow with equal unenthusiasm. There was a smoothness about him, the bland face giving nothing away; only for a moment as he looked at Lady Cecily did something stir in his eyes, but it was gone almost as soon as it came. His coat, which had so pained Mr Anstruther earlier, was obviously well-cut, perhaps fitting his rather heavy figure a little too closely, but there was little to quarrel with. So that it was hard to fathom why, by comparison with the other two gentlemen, he looked so exactly what he was—an odious parvenu.

'Lady Cecily,' his voice was as carefully urbane as his image, 'your father has encouraged me to hope that you will consent to take a drive with me tomorrow in the afternoon. Do tell me that I am not to be disappointed?' The words, seemingly sincere, hung on the air with a curious intensity.

'Oh! I don't think...that is...' Caught at a loss, she cast a vain beseeching glance at the earl.

'What Lady Cecily is endeavouring to explain is that she is already promised to me for tomorrow afternoon,' interposed Mr Anstruther smoothly. 'Another time, perhaps, Mr Elliston.' The fury in the latter's eyes was imperfectly concealed. Mr Anstruther's fingers were encouragingly firm at Cecily's elbow. 'And now, my lord—if you will excuse us, I believe we must seek my aunt, who wishes to take your daughter to sit with Lady Cowper and Lady Sefton. It would hardly do to slight their ladyships, I think?'

Something in the earl's face made Cecily say impulsively, 'I'm sorry, Papa.'

He patted her hand and surprisingly bent to kiss her cheek. 'Go along with you, Cecy. Anstruther's right—mustn't keep the august pillars of society waiting. We'll call on you very soon, eh?'

Having deposited his charge with Aunt Constance, Mr Anstruther went in search of Harry Ireland once more and found him presently seated in a far corner, deep in conversation with an exceedingly modish young lady.

'Eliza!' Mr Anstruther lifted the young lady's outstretched hand fleetingly to his lips, his lazy smile meeting laughing hazel eyes. 'Dame Fortune is undoubtedly with me tonight! I had not hoped to find you here.'

'Go away, Marcus,' said Harry. 'Miss Trent and I have a great deal of catching up to do—and we shall do very much better without you!'

For answer, Mr Anstruther drew up a chair, ostensibly so that Harry would not feel obliged to rise, and disposed himself comfortably. 'I beg you will not heed Major Ireland's lack of company manners, Miss Eliza,' he said in his drollest way, adding indulgently, 'I fear he has been too long amongst the rude soldiery—and then you know his wound is bound to make him shockingly cross-grained.'

The violence of the major's protest led to Miss Trent's assuring him, eyes twinkling, that she had not the least quarrel with his demeanour or his continuing presence.

'There! You see?' The major was triumphant.

'Ah, but it is so like you, ma'am, to seek to set him at ease,' said Mr Anstruther gravely, 'when I am sure you cannot be content to fritter your time away in the company of such a rattle.'

'Better a rattle than a Bond Street fribble!'

Eliza Trent listened to the continuing exchange of pleasantries with undisguised enjoyment. 'Oh, you two! If one did not know you for such friends, one would never suspect how very pleased you are to see one another.'

'That's as maybe,' protested the major, game to the end. 'But a true friend would have the common decency to efface himself when he's been tipped the wink that he ain't wanted!'

'Not so, Harry,' said Mr Anstruther piously. 'A *true friend* is one who is sufficiently forgiving to turn the other cheek when he is treated in a manner that can at best be termed shabby! No, no, dear fellow——' he held up a hand as Harry drew breath '—I will not hear of your apologising. I understand perfectly how it is with you.' The major's indignation dissolved suddenly in a splutter of laughter which brought an answering gleam. 'That's better. Matter of fact, I have need of you—both of you.' He turned to Miss Trent. 'Eliza—have you met my aunt's godchild?'

'Why, yes—at least, we have only spoken briefly as yet...'

'And?'

She looked at Mr Anstruther curiously. 'I like her. She is delightfully unspoiled, but rather shy, I think, though that is perfectly understandable; to be thrust into London life when one has been used to living quietly must be an ordeal for anyone of a sensitive disposition.' She did not mention the earl, though the added embarrassment of his presence could hardly have gone unnoticed. 'I believe I should like to know Lady Cecily better.'

'Splendid. Then will you oblige me by doing just that? In my opinion, the child badly needs a friend, someone of her own sex who is young enough to be the recipient of her confidences and wise enough to guide her through these early days. I cannot think of anyone better fitted to lend her such support.'

The dimples in Miss Trent's cheeks deepened. 'You pay a vastly pretty compliment, sir, but there is no need to turn me up sweet, you know—I shall be very pleased to befriend Lady Cecily, if Lady Wigmore...'

'Oh, you know Aunt Constance...the soul of generosity, but no notion at all of a young girl's needs! One has but to observe Lady Cecily's dress, her hair...' Mr Anstruther's glance damned them briefly before coming to dwell with pleasure upon Miss Trent's fashionably clustered auburn curls, cunningly threaded with ribbons decked with seed pearls. More pearls edged the neck of her elegant half-robe of amber crêpe. 'I'll wager that Friday-faced maid of my aunt's had the say there! It's clear to me that something will have to be done about it quickly—before the Season gets fully under way. The child must be dressed simply, but with much greater imagination, if she is to make sufficient impression upon the world. Accomplish that and you will be rendering her an invaluable service.'

'There is nothing I should enjoy more, but...' Miss Trent still hesitated, not sure how to proceed without indelicacy.

Mr Anstruther, however, was quick to interpret her train of thought. 'There will be no difficulty,' he said carelessly. 'Aunt Constance will stand the blunt.'

'You're being unconscionably busy about your aunt's business, all of a sudden,' said Major Ireland, vastly intrigued. 'What is to be my role in this curious little charade, I wonder? For, if you are thinking to cozen me into squiring Lady Cecily around——' his tone grew odiously complacent '—I must tell you now that I am like to be in great demand over the next few weeks, so I shouldn't care to commit myself to anything of too confining a nature!'

'My dear Harry,' drawled Mr Anstruther, 'I would not presume to ask so much of you. I shall, of course, myself assume the role of escort and mentor to Lady Cecily. But precisely because you are at present enjoying a certain cachet, I would ask you to pay a little extra attention to her—let it be known, in quite a casual way, that you think her the most charming of creatures. That much, surely, would not greatly inconvenience you?'

'It ain't like you to take so much trouble for a chit scarce out of the schoolroom.' The major was by now downright suspicious. 'You're up to something, Marcus! I've known you too long to be gulled *so* easily. Come clean, now—what's your game?'

Mr Anstruther looked mildly astonished. 'Game? My dear Harry, no game, I assure you. I am simply being a dutiful nephew!'

CHAPTER THREE

IT WAS a rather confused young lady who retired to her bedchamber later that evening, having assured her godmother that she had enjoyed her first party very much and that, yes—her nephew had been everything she had said. The old lady had seemed much pleased and promised that this was but a beginning—there were much greater delights in store for her. Both studiously avoided any mention of her father and his companion—or of the Baroness von Oppenheimer.

In her room the candles had been lit, the fire made up, and a ewer of water waited, steaming slightly beside the bowl on the marble stand. The maid, Lizzie, was vigorously engaged in warming the sheets. She looked up with a quick smile, a pleasant rapport having been established between the two young people from the first, her young ladyship having no hoity-toity ways such as might have been expected.

'Nice party, milady?' she ventured.

It seemed that there was a hesitation before Lady Cecily said absently, 'Yes, very nice. Thank you Lizzie, if you would just unhook me, you may go to bed now. You must be tired.'

Lizzie took a closer look at Lady Cecily's face. Still homesick, belike! She remembered how it'd been when she'd first left home. She did as she was bid, murmured, 'Goodnight, milady,' and slipped from the room.

Left alone, Cecily felt little inclination to make preparations for bed. Instead she wandered across to the looking-glass set on a table placed between the room's two windows. A thin shadowy image thrown up by the candlelight stared back at her as though at a stranger.

'Insipid!' she said aloud, just as the baroness had said it as she was leaving—quite clearly, knowing full well that she had been heard. Tugging unsteadily at the pins confining her hair, she shook it into a pale cascade about her face, and, released suddenly from its unwelcome constraint, her scalp made painful protest. 'Oh, stuff!' she muttered in disgust and turned her back on the unflattering reflection.

The windows had wide ledges and on one of these she sat morosely, knees drawn up to make a resting place for her chin. Bella would be mad as fire if she could see what a sad botch her sister was making of things...

'You must make a really splendid match, Cecy, and then I can come to town and you will be able to present me to all your friends!'

The words lay at the back of her mind as a bitter reproach. Bella ought to have been the eldest, of course. She was fashionably dark, and much the prettier, and had never made any secret of the fact that she meant to marry well, 'For I don't intend to stay buried in the country for ever, living in *penury*!' It had been said with all the vehemence of a wilful fifteen-year-old, but Cecily didn't doubt for one moment that she meant every word. It occasionally astonished Cecily to discover how clear-sighted and—yes, it had to be admitted—mercenary Bella was.

'Well, I don't care what you think! Someone in this house has to be practical,' her young sister had declared with a pert toss of dusky curls when Cecily had taken her to task over her attitude to Lady Wigmore's invitation. 'Mama is forever prostrate with the migraine—and you don't seem to care for anything beyond whether we should dig up the east lawns to grow more vegetables when it is quite plain that you have only to get a rich husband and we shan't need to bother about digging up any old lawns!'

Get a rich husband! How simple it sounded—and how crude. Cecily remembered feeling suddenly quite sick at the thought of leaving Churston and Mama. Bella was quite self-sufficient, of course, but there was Cassie, who was nearly thirteen and on the brink of girlhood, and little Mary, who needed so much love and understanding. How would they go on without her? Cecily sighed. If only she could be like Bella, who saw the London visit as a great adventure and had been quite green with jealousy that she wasn't going. They had been alone in the small back parlour at the time, with the most presentable of Cecily's dresses strewn about the chairs, trying, with the aid of some new trimmings and the fashion pages of *The Ladies' Monthly Museum* which Mrs Fitzallen had lent them, to assemble an adequate wardrobe for the forthcoming visit to London. Mama was lying down as usual and the two younger girls were in the schoolroom with Miss Gilbert, who had been their governess forever—though Cecily wondered how much longer they would be able to afford her.

'If you will only put yourself about to be agreeable, Cecy, I dare say you might do very well. You aren't as pretty as me, of course,' Bella went on with sisterly candour, 'but as you're so thin you could try to cultivate an air of genteel fragility—some gentlemen are quite susceptible to that sort of thing, I believe.'

'Bella! As if I could—or indeed, would!'

Her sister's lower lip had been set in a wilful pout. 'Well, you needn't sound so... sanctimonious! If one doesn't have money, one is obliged to use guile. And it can work,' she declared with renewed enthusiasm, 'because I remember reading about three Irish girls who were quite penniless, besides being absolute *nobodies*—and they all married terribly well.'

'You read too many trashy novels,' mumbled Cecily through a mouthful of pins, 'and you know Mama doesn't like you doing so.'

'Oh, but this was *true*. Of course,' Bella conceded, 'it was some time ago and they were all great beauties, but it does prove it can be done! Just so long as you don't go falling in love with someone totally unsuitable...' This was greeted with an unintelligible squeak. 'Oh, you can protest all you like, but *I* know how idiotishly romantical you can be. Why, you went around in a positive daze for weeks when Mrs Fitzallen's nephew came to stay—and he had no expectations at all, besides being only the second officer of a brig!'

'Now *you're* being silly!' Cecily had protested, wishing that she didn't colour up so easily. 'I was barely sixteen at the time and James Fitzallen was *very* handsome.' She spread out her favourite morning dress on the floor and experimented with two different lengths of braid. Perhaps the blond ribbon would be best after all...

'Lord, Cecy! You're never taking that old blue muslin. It's too shabby for anything! Anyhow, I don't know why you are going to so much trouble when Lady Wigmore is almost certain to deck you out with a new wardrobe.'

But *that* Cecily wouldn't allow to be likely. She had, after all, her new blue pelisse—and her best bonnet might well pass for new if freshly trimmed with blue ribbons. Besides which, she now had two brand-new evening gowns to swell her meagre store, thanks to dear Mrs Fitzallen, who had given her those two lengths of twilled silk which she vowed she had bought quite by mistake, though Cecily suspected otherwise.

Bella, however, had refused to share her views, a close perusal of the society columns of *The Ladies' Monthly Museum* having convinced her that, short of Lady Wigmore's turning out to be an unstylish freak or worse still not the person of standing in fashionable circles that Mama had assured them she was, a mere two or three new dresses—and homemade ones at that—would prove totally inadequate to meet the needs of a London Season.

Her sister's utterances, however, prophetic as they had been, in no way prepared Cecily for the majestic elegance of the house in Portland Place—or for Lady Wigmore herself, whose formidable proportions and odd, freakish manners were at first sight alarming. The realisation that Lady Wigmore, in spite of her eccentricities, was used to moving in first circles, and that her life was likely to become an unremitting round of balls and breakfasts, routs and assemblies, had filled Cecily with alarm. She could only hope to learn quickly how to go on so that she might not disgrace her benefactress, whose massive bosom, she had soon discovered, concealed a good and kindly heart.

Cecily stretched her legs out before her and regarded her toes pensively. Bella, of course, would have taken Lady Wigmore's high-nosed friends in her stride. She certainly wouldn't have told Mr Anstruther that she didn't wish for his approbation! Cecily blushed, remembering. In the circumstances, she was bound to admit that he had behaved a great deal better than she deserved. That he was helping her in order to please his aunt must not be allowed to weigh with her, for she could not afford to indulge the sin of pride! She had not the least doubt that Mr Anstruther could achieve anything he set his mind to. He certainly had an excellent opinion of himself, but she supposed that was quite allowable when one looked as he did—and if people were so silly as to set great store by what he said and did the fault was surely as much theirs as his! For herself she thought she might grow to like him rather well. He had certainly saved her from being obliged to drive with Mr Elliston, which circumstance alone must earn him her gratitude, and he had introduced her, besides, to several of his friends. In fact, if only she could become used to seeing from her window, as now, an unending panorama of rooftops guarded by rows of tall, regimented chimney pots, in place of the raggle-taggle flowerbeds and lawns of home, she might even come to enjoy her stay—and if Mr Anstruther were to find her an *agreeable* husband...

She slept surprisingly well that night and woke to find Lizzie throwing back the curtains to reveal a blue sky and sunshine dappling the high rococo ceiling.

Lady Wigmore was not an early riser, but Cecily could not bear to lie abed once she was awake. It was very strange having so little to occupy her time, but already her mornings had assumed a pattern. She breakfasted alone in the little morning parlour and then, to while away the time until Lady Wigmore should put in an appearance, she had formed the habit of repairing to the music-room. This delightful room—small, high, and octagonal in shape—looked rather as though it had been squashed between its neighbours. The walls were panelled with frescoes much concerned with entwined lovers, and among the few choice items of furniture was a spinet made of walnut exquisitely inlaid with tulipwood. Here she had been able to pass many a pleasant hour. So engrossed was she on this morning, however, that it came as something of a shock when a pause in her recital was greeted with the polite patter of applause.

'A delightful study, Lady Cecily,' said Mr Anstruther, advancing across the room to lean on the spinet. From the satirical inflexion in his voice she was unsure whether he was passing an opinion on her performance or her looks, but a moment's reflection showed her the absurdity of construing the remark as anything beyond a meaningless pleasantry. She sprang up, very much aware that the blue muslin which had merited Bella's scorn was indeed shabby in spite of the new blond ribbons, and that with her hair caught back in a matching ribbon and hanging almost to her shoulders she looked and felt like a schoolroom miss.

'I hadn't expected anyone s-so early.'

'Ah, but I am not *anyone*,' he reminded her, plainly amused by her confusion. 'That was a charming little song. Do you play as well as you sing, I wonder? Sit down again if you please and play something for me. A little Bach, perhaps?'

Did he think her incapable? Accepting the challenge, she came back to the spinet and, very conscious of his close scrutiny, proceeded to render one of the early preludes at a pace which would have sent Miss Gilbert into an apoplexy. The last note died away into silence.

And into the silence came Mr Anstruther's voice, at its drollest. 'An interesting interpretation, Lady Cecily. A shade too much bravura for my taste, but I dare say that can be corrected with practice.'

Cecily had the grace to blush. Then she laughed and rallied valiantly under his quizzical eye. 'It was appalling,' she confessed frankly. 'I can do very much better, I promise you. The trouble is, you see, that I occasionally grow quite wilful when I am driven to defend myself.'

'Do you, indeed? I am obliged to you for telling me—I shall strive to bear it in mind.' Mr Anstruther straightened up. 'Well now, my pugnacious infant, before this house becomes infested with visitors to whom one must be polite, do you think you could bring your mind to the contemplation of your future? You are still of a mind to accept my help?'

'Yes, of course, sir.' She looked at him half shyly. 'That is . . . if *you* are sure. I w-wondered if you might not have thought better of your offer?'

He didn't answer, but one eyebrow lifted interrogatively as she hurried on, 'Well, it would be perfectly understandable. Lady Wigmore cannot have expected so much of you and I c-cannot see why you should w-wish to put yourself to so much trouble for me!'

Mr Anstruther studied the earnest young face turned up to him. With almost anyone else he would have found such a speech instantly suspect, but she was quite without guile. He smiled faintly.

'Let us call it a whim.'

Cecily wasn't sure that she favoured being at the mercy of a whim. Her uncertainty must have showed.

'Lady Cecily,' he chided gently, 'I have devoted a long and sleepless night to the consideration of your affairs. It would be churlish in the extreme an' you threw such industry back in my face!'

It was sometimes difficult to know when he was quizzing. She said, polite as a child, 'You are very kind.'

'Am I?' He frowned, her words jarring on him suddenly. Kindness surely implied selflessness—generosity, even. Were his motives so pure, or was he simply amusing himself? The thought made him uncomfortable. He put it from him and began instead to talk of the need to do something drastic about her wardrobe.

She was quick to assure him that she had brought quite eight dresses with her, three of which were as yet unworn. He lifted his quizzing glass to examine the blue muslin. His silence, more explicit than words, suggested that they had much better remain so.

'I have spoken to Aunt Constance,' he continued, 'and she is more than ready to see you fitted out in prime twig...'

'Oh, no! I really can't! S-such an imposition...when she has been so good to me already...'

'And is enjoying every minute! Mr dear child, you must *know* that?' He came and took her hands, lifting her to her feet. 'My aunt is grown very fond of you. Do allow her to prove as much. She has never until now had anyone upon whom to lavish her attentions—except me, in my youth.' His lazy smile deepened. 'And I was ever an ungrateful brat!'

Cecily could not conceive of a gentleman of his elegance ever having been a brat, but had not quite the courage to say so.

Lady Wigmore's reactions were very much as Mr Anstruther had predicted, her only quarrel being with herself for not having taken steps sooner, 'For depend upon it, child, this house will soon be turned upside down with callers—and the invitations... Why, the mantelshelf is already becoming littered with them. Marcus is quite right... there isn't a moment to be lost.'

It seemed to Cecily that the next few days were an unending stream of comings and goings. Lady Cowper called personally to bring vouchers for Almack's and was charming. Her papa called several times, never staying long enough to provoke the caustic edge of Lady Wigmore's tongue, but seemingly dogged by the necessity to reassure himself that Cecy was happy and did not hold him to blame for having shirked his responsibilities. He appeared less heartened than might have been supposed by his daughter's ingenuous expectation that, 'Things may all turn out for the best, you know, for Mr Anstruther has decided to bring me into fashion and has great hopes of f-finding me a suitable husband...'

It was amid all this activity that Cecily was introduced to the extraordinarily complex world of dressmakers and hairdressers and the like, to which any aspiring young lady of fashion must, it seemed, submit herself. That it was on the whole a joyous rather than a trying experience was almost entirely due to Eliza Trent, whose warm smile and unaffected manners had instantly dispelled the awe which Cecily had felt upon first meeting this exceedingly modish young lady. The two were soon fast friends and Lady Wigmore was more than content to entrust the refurbishing of her protégée to Miss Trent's faultless taste. Her nephew, also, having done what she had initially asked of him, showed no immediate inclination to bow out of the enterprise.

Cecily supposed that Mr Anstruther was acting out of politeness when he escorted them to the exclusive showrooms of Madame Louise in Bruton Street. Only as the carriage halted did she realise that he meant to come in with them. A startled glance at Eliza brought only a gurgle of laughter and a whispered, 'It is quite proper, my love!' And indeed, Madame Louise greeted him with so much deferential familiarity that Cecily was driven to the conclusion that he must be a not-infrequent visitor to her establishment, which raised all kinds of conjectures sufficient to cause a blush, the more so as she looked up at that moment to encounter his satirical eye.

But her embarrassment was soon forgotten in the luxury of her surroundings. All the way coming in the carriage she had resolved to be sensible; if she must have new dresses, they should be chosen with an eye to practicality—Lady Wigmore's money must not be frittered away on unnecessary or extravagant purchases.

Madame Louise seemed to share her view as she gushed, 'There must be nothing of a sophisticated nature for the young *mademoiselle*, I think. Such a fairness, so slim and graceful a figure demands only the flimsiest of materials, the most delicate of colours in order that one preserves an air of fragility...' Cecily was obliged to repress a smile as she recalled Bella's advice.

But the time spent poring over the fashion pages of *The Ladies' Monthly Museum* with Bella had taught Cecily more than she had realised. It soon became quite clear to her that not only was this bewildering array of gowns being paraded for her delectation totally impractical—every one of them was also almost certainly ruinously expensive! But they were so beautiful that she lost her head, scarcely demurring as Eliza bade her try first one and then another, deferring occasionally to Mr Anstruther, who protested that he was but an observer while subjecting each garment to a devastatingly critical appraisal. She could almost have gone on her knees to him when he approved a dearly coveted redingote fashioned of palest grey twilled sarsenet, and trimmed all down the front with pink braid. When later he lazily reproved her partiality for a totally unsuitable ball gown in cerise satin with an embroidered half-train, she was philosophical, for she had just glimpsed the dress that Madame Louise was carrying—a diaphanous confection of blue gauze embroidered all over with tiny silver harebells.

Only as she was being buttoned into her own pelisse again did Cecily come down to earth with a jolt upon hearing Eliza say with a sigh, 'Oh, my dear, you will turn heads for sure!' She turned in dismay to behold the vast quantity of morning gowns, evening gowns, half-robes, tippets and shawls, pelisses, bonnets, and all manner of gewgaws being set to one side by Madame's assistants.

Horror now uppermost, she murmured weakly, 'But... we c-cannot possibly have purchased *so* many things?'

'Oh, this is but a beginning!' Eliza assured her blithely. 'One could scarcely contemplate a London Season with less. Is that not so, Marcus?'

Mr Anstruther agreed, watching curiously the young face that was so revealing. She had been all this while like a child playing at dressing up, a faint colour touching her cheekbones, her eyes brilliant with excitement. And now had come a look almost of guilt. It made him wonder, remembering her story, just how much of a novelty this morning's excursion had been.

But he had no way of knowing the full extent of the struggle going on inside her. She wanted desperately to possess all these lovely clothes, but years of making over, of adding flounces and re-furbishing lace, had left her with a strong frugal streak which must deem so much extravagance almost sinful. In all of her eighteen years she had not *seen* so many dresses. Out of sheer habit she even fell to assessing how splendidly she could outfit the whole family from just a small part of her new wardrobe while Madame Louise, unaware of this speculative violation of her creations, was all sharp-faced complaisance. Cecily, much embarrassed, hastily averted her eyes, lest Madame divine the train her thoughts were taking, and thus found her attention caught by a shimmer of pink lace.

On a little stand in one corner of the salon a parasol reposed, the body impeccably pleated, the ferrule a slim shining point, and the long silver handle rising elegantly from a provocative froth of pink lace. In a morning filled with beautiful things, this was without doubt the most exquisite! She must have sighed aloud, for her companions exchanged amused glances.

'Do you fancy that scrap of nonsense?' drawled Mr Anstruther.

'Oh, no!' Cecily jumped and coloured up, deeply ashamed to be discovered in contemplation of anything so frivolous. 'That is . . . no, of course not!' she concluded resolutely, and wished he wouldn't look at her in quite that way. She said firmly, 'I cannot think what Lady Wigmore will say to all this as it is!'

'I very much hope,' said Mr Anstruther, 'that she will commend us upon a morning well spent.'

CHAPTER FOUR

SPRING had come to London; the great frost which had held the city in so violent a grip that a fair had sprung up on the frozen River Thames was now but a distant memory. The war was over and a festive mood prevailed. White cockades, Bourbon tokens, fleur-de-lys sprouted everywhere amid the burgeoning green trees. The sun shone on pavements busy with spent blossom which scurried along in snowy drifts and floated down between iron railings to wither away unseen on basement steps.

With the spring came the cream of fashionable society, girded for another London Season, eager to entertain and be entertained, to indulge in a surfeit of pleasure. Once more at five o'clock each afternoon the park was thronged with carriages, with people strolling at their ease, and all with one purpose—to observe and to be observed.

It was here, Mr Anstruther decided, that Cecily should make her first public appearance in his company. She had been to several small assemblies with his aunt and was already the object of a little gentle speculation. There were, he knew, any number of invitations arriving at Portland Place for the opening balls of the Season, more than sufficient to please Lady Wigmore, but he was not so easily satisfied.

Cecily was ready for their drive well before the hour appointed by Mr Anstruther. She went to the Chinese room to show herself to Lady Wigmore, who had accepted with cheerful equanimity the arrival at her door of quantities of bandboxes filled with clothes and fal-lals without the least regard to their cost, content simply to approve each new creation as it was revealed.

'Very fetching, child!' boomed her ladyship as the slim girl twirled obediently at her command. 'How clever of you to choose a grey which so exactly matches your eyes. A nice, youthful bonnet, too...the pink lining gives that pale little face of yours quite a becoming glow!'

'Dear Aunt Constance,' drawled Mr Anstruther from the doorway, 'you had ever a pretty way with a compliment!'

He had arrived unannounced and was strolling now across the room in his unhurried way, enveloped in a drab driving coat with more capes than Cecily could possibly count. He made his aunt a leg and regarded Cecily in an amiably critical manner.

Lady Wigmore shrugged off the implied criticism. 'Cecy knows my blunt tongue well enough by now not to take offence, eh, child?'

Cecily hastened to reassure her.

Mr Anstruther seemed to frown. 'You know, seeing that ensemble again, I am not sure that it doesn't lack a certain . . . something?'

She was taken aback. Their friendship had advanced to the point where she was quite used to being teased, and she listened for the dry note in that voice she was beginning to know so well; not hearing it, she was outraged.

'But you approved the dress! You even suggested that I wear it!'

'Did I?' He stood pensively, one hand behind his back, his quizzing glass raised. 'Yes. Well, it is as Aunt Constance remarked, very fetching! But this, I venture to think——' he withdrew the hand from behind his back '—will make it the more so!'

It was the pink parasol. She was deprived of words. Blushing under the scrutiny of his now laughing eyes, she took it from him almost reverently.

'I have never owned anything half so . . . so beautiful!' she sighed. 'Oh, but I'm not sure if I should . . . if it is proper . . .' She looked to Lady Wigmore, unaware of the naked pleading in the look. 'Ought I to accept such a gift, ma'am?'

Lady Wigmore gave her nephew a very old-fashioned look which he returned with blandness. 'Lord, gel, I don't see why not, if you've a fancy for such fripperies! It ain't much to my taste, but as a present it seems quite unexceptionable.

Anyhow, you and Marcus are as near related as bedamned.'

'Beautifully put!' murmured Mr Anstruther, unrepentant.

Cecily was handed up into Mr Anstruther's curricle and settled herself before carefully opening the parasol. She gave it an experimental twirl and was content. Mr. Anstruther glanced at her as he took up the reins and ordered his groom to let go the horses' heads. Her pleasure in the gift was so delightedly unfeigned that it would be churlish to confess that he had devised its employment quite cold-bloodedly as but one more stratagem in his bid to bring her into prominence, a stratagem whose success seemed assured, for even without the parasol Lady Cecily was now eminently presentable—with it, she would undoubtedly turn all heads!

The horses were still very fresh and Cecily was quite happy to remain silent, admiring his skill with the ribbons, until they were well under way. Then Mr Anstruther glanced down at her.

'You are very quiet.'

'I thought you would prefer it. I know Ben hated one to chatter when he was trying to cope with high-couraged horses. Not,' she added, frankly appraising, 'that he ever owned any half so fine as your chestnuts.'

'Do you drive?'

'A little—but nothing grander than a gig and a placid old mare.'

The comparison drew a faint smile. 'Ben used to let me take the ribbons on his Tilbury when he was in a good mood, though.' She gave the chestnuts a speculative glance. 'I suppose you wouldn't care to have me drive your team?'

'You suppose rightly, infant.' He was crushingly unequivocal. But as she gave her philosophical little shrug, he said with more sympathy, 'Your brother's death must have been a great grief to you?'

'Yes, for he was the most splendid brother! But it was so much worse for Mama, you know. He was her firstborn, besides being her only son. She d-doted on him and I doubt that she will ever recover from the loss.' A frown troubled her brow. 'I do w-worry about her...'

'But there are others, are there not? Is not your sister very competent?'

'Oh, yes!' Cecily said quickly, striving to be fair. 'Bella will cope very well. It is only that she d-doesn't understand Mama quite as I do.'

Doesn't spoil her, more like, thought Mr Anstruther with perception, but he said only, 'And your other sisters?'

'Cassie is barely thirteen and a dreamer. She is going to be the beauty of the family. And Mary...' How did one explain Mary, who had never spoken or cried in all her six years? Cecily felt her throat constrict with the recollection of Mary running down the front steps on the morning she had left home, clinging to her in silent convulsive misery. She found Mr Anstruther regarding her in some curiosity, and said a little thickly, 'Something went wrong when Mary was born. I d-don't perfectly understand the reasons, but Mama lost several babies after Cassie... and Mary's was a very difficult birth...'

It occurred to her that this was not at all the kind of thing one spoke about to a gentleman during an afternoon promenade, but Mr Anstruther didn't appear to find the conversation incongruous—or, if he did, he was too polite to show it.

'You miss them all, don't you?' he said abruptly.

'Yes, I do—quite dreadfully!' she confessed, and continued with resolution, 'And that, you see, is why I must make the very b-best marriage I can, as soon as I can, so that I can look after them all properly. And you know——' she looked about her eagerly as they swept in through the park gate '—although I didn't really want to come to London at all, I think I might enjoy it rather well!'

There were plenty of people already taking the air and progress was, of necessity, slow. Mr Anstruther was greeted on all sides and halted several times to introduce his charming companion, who was, as he had hoped, attracting a not inconsiderable amount of attention.

A stylish lady in a stationary barouche had just bade farewell to a small riding party and, seeing

Mr Anstruther, lifted a gloved hand in greeting. He brought the curricle alongside and once again introductions were effected.

Lady Jersey's restless eyes took in every detail of the delicate features so becomingly framed beneath the pink parasol. So this was Camden's girl! A nondescript little thing, the baroness had said, but there was nothing nondescript about this creature with the lavender-grey eyes. She had an untouched quality about her that most women would give their souls to possess, but was not, one would have thought, the kind of female to appeal to the eminently sophisticated Mr Anstruther, whose tastes usually ran to more voluptuous charms. Lady Jersey transferred her gaze to his buttonhole, now devoid of its floral tribute. Well, well.

'We have seen nothing of you this two weeks past, Mr Anstruther,' she said playfully. 'Certain of your acquaintances have wondered at your prolonged absence.'

He gave her a faint appreciative smile. 'I felt the need for a change, my dear ma'am. You will understand, I am sure.'

'Oh, I do indeed!' Lady Jersey glanced again at the shy girl beside him and her voice was heavy with satire. 'Perhaps there is something in the air, for Madame Devine seems to have been driven by the same need. She has deserted us in favour of Paris. Did you know?' She uttered a high-pitched little laugh. 'Everyone talks of going there now that the

Corsican tyrant is finally vanquished. Louis the Gouty is all eagerness to quit our shores so that he may restore the Bourbon succession. I really think I must make the journey myself before very long...strange how Paris draws one!' She leaned forward to tap on the coachman's box, saying as the coach swayed in motion, 'Lady Wigmore has received vouchers for Almack's, I believe?' And with a gracious inclination of the head, 'We shall look forward to seeing you there, Lady Cecily.'

'What a strange, restless sort of lady,' said Cecily diffidently. 'Does she always chatter so?'

'Always. Did you dislike her? Many people do. Her enemies call her Silence!'

'How unkind!' Her instant sympathy drew from him a smile, so that she was encouraged to pursue the conversation. 'One hears so much about Almack's—is it truly as grand as it sounds?'

'It is so exclusive,' he told her in his drollest manner, 'that to be seen there is everything! It matters not one whit that the rooms are commonplace, the refreshments diabolically insipid, and the company frequently so dull beyond measure that were it not such a challenge to one's ego to gain admittance I doubt any of us would bother to go at all.'

Cecily gave him a suspicious look. 'You are funning?'

'No—on my life!'

'Well!' Her tone was reproving. 'It sounds to me like a shocking bore—besides being a nonsensical waste of time!'

This made him laugh out loud. Several people turned, curious to learn who had prompted the urbane Mr Anstruther to such a degree of animation.

'Oh, it is, indeed, infant—lamentably so!' And with a quick teasing glance, 'Poor Cecy! Am I destroying all your illusions?'

Her cheeks grew unaccountably warm, but she was saved from answer by the happy sight of Eliza in an immensely stylish bonnet and pelisse walking along beside the tan with Major Ireland. The curricle was halted, the reins given over to the groom, and Cecily was helped down, to be greeted enthusiastically by her friend.

'Cecy! That is *the* parasol. Marcus bought it for you, did he not?' Eliza turned to Mr Anstruther. 'It is exactly what was needed. How clever of you to see it!' And to Major Ireland, 'Harry, doesn't Cecy look quite perfect?'

The major eyed curiously the young girl, who had gone rather quiet, then, taking her hand, carried it gallantly to his lips. 'Quite perfect,' he agreed.

'Of course, what you must do now, my love, is to have a matching one for each of your ensembles. Am I not right, Marcus?' Eliza prattled on.

He lifted a quizzical eyebrow. 'As ever, my dear, your judgement is impeccable. It shall be done.'

'Will no one ask Lady Cecily what she thinks?' said Harry Ireland, still watching her. 'How do you say, ma'am?' he rallied her gently. 'Do you not think these two vastly busy, arranging your affairs with so little regard for your wishes?'

Cecily dragged her thoughts back from the sad reflection that her lovely pink parasol had been selected with the same detached consideration as the rest of her finery. And she had thought it a particular gift! Three pairs of eyes were on her, awaiting an answer, Mr. Anstruther's in particular a little questioning. How green he would think her if he knew her thoughts. She put up her chin a fraction.

'Oh, I don't mind,' she said gaily. 'I'm sure it is a s-splendid idea... if only Lady Wigmore approves.'

Lady Wigmore did approve, of course, though she didn't know what to make of it all. To be sure, it was very gratifying to be every night invited to some function or other, to see Cecy at the centre of attention, and to hear her friend Mrs Longford, describe her as, 'A very prettily behaved creature... not in the least puffed-up or inclined to put herself forward as many would do, I'm sure, in her position! Your nephew paying her such attentions as he does!'

And she had chuckled when her goddaughter related a meeting with the Baroness von Oppenheimer and how that lady's discreetly plucked eyebrows had all but vanished into her hennaed hair upon registering Cecily's transformation. Cecy had quite innocently, and in some awe, revealed that Marcus had put Tilly down well and truly, letting her know in the politest way imaginable that if she expected to see him at her assembly she must also invite his aunt and Lady Cecily.

It was all and more than she had hoped for when she had first solicited Marcus's help, and yet she was not entirely easy—perhaps because she no longer felt herself to be quite in control of the situation. And—a bitter pill to swallow this—with all the racketing around, she was beginning to feel her age. She had forgotten how tiring it could all be. Still, who better to keep an eye on the child than her nephew, since he seemed willing enough? And if, as seemed likely, Cecily became a *succès fou*, she was sensible enough not to let it go to her head.

Cecily quickly became known as 'the girl with the parasol,' Mr Anstruther's device for bringing her to the notice of society having succeeded beyond all expectation.

'It's very flattering, of course,' she admitted, pink-cheeked, when first she heard of it. 'But it cannot last, for there are so many young ladies of the very first stare, you know, who are able to display a parasol with far more elegance than I could ever achieve.'

Yet it was her total lack of studied elegance which set Cecily apart. She combined all the most endearing qualities of youth with a refreshingly honest personality, and, as she grew in confidence, many a gentleman, weary of duplicity and artifice, was tempted to try if he could win her regard.

She was soon able to write home to Mama in the most glowing terms of Lady Wigmore's kindness to her, of the splendid time she was enjoying and how many beaux were vying with each other for the privilege of escorting her to some ball or rout—'Though Mr Anstruther does not think any of them to be worthy of consideration.' For Bella's benefit she included details of all her prettiest gowns and the parasols and lots of descriptions of personages of importance, including the Prince Regent, whom she was sad to say she found extremely stout: 'Lady Wigmore is to present me at one of the Queen's drawing-rooms which has put me in a quake, but Mr Anstruther says I shall do very well and he knows a great deal about such things.' And then, aware that her letter was overburdened with frivolities, she assured her mama that she was ever mindful of the true purpose of her visit and that she had no intention of succumbing entirely to the hollow pursuits of pleasure. 'I see Papa quite regularly,' she concluded, and, mentally crossing her fingers, added, 'and he sends to you all his very best love.' Having sent her own dearest love to them all, especially to little Mary, Cecily sat back with a sigh, mangling the pen until it was quite beyond mending as she fell suddenly prey to homesickness. Life was so much simpler at Churston. She feared that her present life was encouraging in her certain tendencies which she must deplore. For example, no one at home would ever have thought her devious, yet she had not been quite honest with Mama. She had not mentioned Mr Pendle, who was the most recent and most promising of her admirers, or the less-favoured, but more prestigious Marquis of Bayldon, whom Harry had facetiously termed 'a doubtful starter'.

'Oh, I don't mind.' She had smiled kindly at Harry as his flippancy earned him a quelling look from Mr Anstruther. Her friendship with Harry had developed quite naturally as she and Eliza grew close. He was so like her brother Ben, with the same teasing sense of humour, that she soon found herself treating him in very much the same fashion. Between the three of them a silly kind of game had developed which they called 'Finding a rich husband for Cecily'. Somehow, reduced to a game, it didn't seem quite so awful. Mr Anstruther tolerated their idiocy in his rather languid way, but seldom participated, and Cecily sometimes had the distinct feeling that he didn't approve.

Mr Pendle's name came up again on the day the four of them went to Richmond. The outing had been proposed by Harry, who wished to try riding further than the park. His wound was much improved, and though he still relied on a stick his limp was now transformed into a kind of rolling, swashbuckling swagger. Eliza, he suggested, should drive Cecily in her phaeton and the two gentlemen would ride.

As an outing, it was a great success, for what could be more agreeable than a pleasant day spent in the company of friends? The gentlemen were handsome, the young ladies complemented each other in looks; Eliza, dashing in green velvet, a hat with a swirling feather displaying her auburn curls to advantage, and Cecily, a slight figure in a close-fitting bonnet, her fair undressed curls tumbling on to the shoulders of a sprigged muslin dress of palest pink, and carrying her parasol.

'Y'know, we're a lucky pair of dogs!' exclaimed Harry as he dismounted and came to help the girls down from their carriage. Cecily noticed at once that his limp was more pronounced and that he was looking a little white about the mouth. She exchanged a quick look with the others and Mr Anstruther suggested casually that the sun had dried the grass out quite well enough to put down the rugs they had brought. They rested for a while before taking a little gentle exercise in the sunshine. Then they took down the picnic basket and dined in great style off lobster patties, cold chicken, and wine, after which Harry sat propped against a tree with a sigh and slept. Mr Anstruther lay flat on his back among the rugs, with his ankles neatly crossed and his hat over his eyes, while the two girls fell to gossiping in low tones, stifling a giggle now and then as they talked of the Baroness von Oppenheimer's assembly when she had been thrown into a quake by her son's evident partiality for Cecily, and Lady Wigmore enjoying every minute!

'As if I could ever hold the baron in anything but revulsion!' Cecily shuddered, thus reminded of the middle-aged dandy, well-corseted against the worst ravages of over-indulgence but unable to hide the generous folds of his chin, pushed painfully into prominence by the fashionably high points of his collar. 'He has moist eyes!' she concluded, as if that explained all.

'Whereas Lord Bayldon's are not moist, but uncomfortably knowing,' said Eliza. 'He has a reputation for dalliance, that one.'

'He's a gambler, too,' said Harry, opening his eyes with a snap, refreshed and looking more like a mischievous schoolboy with his black hair in disarray than a soldier who had seen untold horrors. 'I've told you, I think he'll shy off when it comes to the sticking point.' He waggled his stick at Cecily. 'Now this young sprig Pendle's a much safer bet. Excellent temperament . . . taken the bit like a good un! Only waiting for the office to start. Shouldn't think he'll even need a touch of the whip!' He grinned. 'Have you leading him by the nose in no time, I shouldn't wonder!'

Cecily giggled, not sure that she wanted a man she could lead by the nose.

'Don't be coarse, Harry!' Mr Anstruther's voice came austerely from under the brim of his hat. 'If you must extol Mr Pendle's virtues, which I feel are overrated, then I'd as lief you would do so without resorting to the language of the turf! Personally, I feel Cecy could do a lot better.'

The reproof, and the manner of its delivery, proved too much for the other three, who dissolved in whoops of laughter. Mr Anstruther removed his hat with a sigh and sat up gracefully, regarding them in turn with the hint of a smile in the lazy green eyes.

'Well, my children?' he drawled. 'You are pleased to be amused?'

'You were so f-funny! All prone dignity upon the grass!' gasped Cecily.

'Ah!' he said, tolerant of their unbridled mirth.

They continued to discuss Mr Algernon Pendle, who had caused something of a stir when he had arrived in town recently, possessed of a considerable fortune inherited from a distant relation. His background, as far as anyone knew, though unexceptional, was sound, and he could claim Lord Sidmouth for his patron. He had immediately become the target for every matchmaking mama with daughters to bestow, but he would look at none of them. For Mr Pendle had had the good fortune to be riding in the park on the afternoon of Cecily's very first drive, and he had at once been pierced by Cupid's dart.

It had taken him some days to gain an introduction, since when he had taken to haunting her steps, so tiresomely eager, so earnest, but with little conversation beyond a few stumbling pleasantries.

'And he has no chin, my love!' Eliza exclaimed skittishly. 'You cannot possibly wed a man with no chin!'

Cecily acknowledged this to be a considerable impediment, but upon reflection pointed out with sweet gravity that it would be less than kind in her to reject Mr Pendle solely because of a physical peculiarity over which he had no control. She also felt, but did not say, that a mere physical defect might prove infinitely preferable to failings of a more daunting nature and that, placed as she was, it ill-behoved her to be so nice in her notions!

As though he read her thoughts, Mr Anstruther said, 'That fellow Elliston hasn't bothered you lately, has he?'

'Elliston? That mushroom!' cried Harry. 'Good God! He hasn't had the impertinence to try and foist his attentions on you?'

'N-no,' said Cecily evasively. 'But Mr Anstruther c-cut him in the park last week. He rode right up to us, obviously w-wanting to speak, and we drove straight past him. I had expected him to come after us and make a scene!'

'Even he wouldn't be such a clunch as to tangle with Marcus!'

Cecily was painfully aware that Mr Anstruther was watching her. She couldn't bring herself to tell him how angry Papa had been, or that when he had taken her out himself later in the week they had in fact met Mr Elliston. She was sure it had been arranged. It was hard to be rational about her reactions to Mr Elliston—he had said or done nothing out of place—in fact, he had been almost overbearingly polite; it was just an instinctive feeling that behind that smooth face with its too-fair eyebrows and eyelashes there was something infinitely repellent.

It was a great relief to her when the subject was allowed to drop and the rest of the day passed very pleasantly.

CHAPTER FIVE

WHEN Mr Anstruther called upon his aunt one afternoon and found that Mr Pendle had at last plucked up the courage to ask Cecily out for a drive, he cut his visit short and went instead to an elegant house in Grosvenor Square. There, in the upstairs drawing-room, he found his sister reclining upon a sofa in a mood of gentle melancholy which lifted at once upon seeing him. Lady Hester Lambton was a shapely, languorous brunette much indulged by a husband in whose eyes she could do no wrong, and adored by her three children.

'Marcus! What a delightful surprise!'

She extended both hands in welcome, and as he bent to kiss her, eyes as green as his own smiled their pleasure.

'I heard you were back in town, Het. You're looking well. Country life agrees with you.'

'Don't!' she implored him in mock horror. 'I found two freckles this morning, my dear—yes, *two*—I swear it! And as if that were not enough, I haven't a thing to wear and Sir Timothy is quite set upon taking me to the opera this evening!' She bared a slender foot and gave it a speculative wiggle. 'I have been wondering whether or not to paint my toenails gold and wear that Egyptian dress I had from Madame Louise at New Year. What do you think, Marcus?'

Mr Anstruther, who knew well enough that she had whole closets filled with dresses, grinned amiably and sat down beside her.

'I think you will look deliciously decadent and shock all the more respectable theatregoers!'

'Good! You have quite decided me! Now, tell me all the latest *on-dits*.'

But mention of Madame Louise had recalled him to the purpose of his visit. 'Later,' he promised. 'Het, how many eligible young men do you know?'

Hester opened her beautiful eyes very wide. 'What a very odd sort of question—and one I should think you can answer far better than I. Besides which, I can't imagine why you should wish to know.'

'It's really quite simple, my dear. I want you to give a ball to which you will invite all the most agreeable gentlemen of your acquaintance who might conceivably come into that category.' While she was still recovering from this extraordinarily odd request, he added casually, 'I also want you to pay a visit to Aunt Constance.'

'No, really, Marcus—this is a great deal too bad of you! A ball is one thing. I dare say I shall be giving one soon, in any case, though why you can't arrange your own affairs I'm sure I don't know! But visit that old dragon!' Hester made a face.

'When you must remember how she has always terrified me!'

'Gammon!' scoffed her unfeeling brother. 'You have never been terrified in your life—least of all by Aunt Constance.'

'Well, but she makes me feel totally inadequate...and frivolous...'

'You are frivolous, my dear Het!'

She gave a sudden trill of laughter, not unpleased by this pleasantry. 'But why must I go and see her? Is she ill?'

He explained about Lady Wigmore's godchild and how he had become involved in the delicate business of seeing her suitably established. His sister, vastly intrigued, made a point of calling in at Portland Place the very next day and came away looking thoughtful.

'I was never more astonished, dearest!' she confided to Sir Timothy later. 'Why, she is a complete innocent...not beautiful, precisely, but there is a certain quality in her. She has quite the loveliest eyes, and hair the colour of woodsmoke that someone...I suspect Signor Franzioni, for one can almost always discern his touch...has coaxed into the most artless curls...'

'She sounds delightful, my love,' said her adoring husband, teasing. 'I cannot wait to make her acquaintance!'

'Well, you won't have to,' she said cordially, not one whit disturbed by this apparent show of interest, 'for I have invited her to take tea with me tomorrow. Of course, I had to ask Aunt Constance as well, but there is so much more I want to know about Lady Cecily! She is not Marcus's style in the least and you must admit that he is not in the ordinary way given to purely altruistic gestures. Why, when I only suggested to him a while since that he might care to take Henry to Astley's, he was quite short with me!'

It was in the mind of her large genial husband to point out that there was all the difference in the world between taking an unbreeched nevvy to Astley's Circus and paying court to a pretty girl, but in the end he thought better of it.

Cecily enjoyed her visit to Grosvenor Square very much. She liked Sir Timothy quite as well as Lady Hester, and, to the latter's surprise, asked most particularly if she might see the children. Thus Sir Timothy was left to entertain Lady Wigmore while his wife carried Cecily off to the nursery, where she spent quite half an hour playing with them under the indulgent eye of their nanny and showing herself so much at ease with them that it was clear how much she was missing her own family.

Hester took the opportunity while they were away from Lady Wigmore to quiz her with considerable thoroughness and Cecily, all unsuspecting, obliged her by chattering in her usual open way as they conversed in the most amiable terms.

Sir Timothy was surprised, therefore, to find his wife in pensive mood when the visitors had left. 'I thought Lady Cecily quite charming,' he ventured.

'Oh, she is!' Hester chewed on her lip. 'And I am in a positive ferment of indecision. Dearest, what am I to do? Lady Cecily doesn't want for sense, in spite of her youth, but I was watching her most particularly and . . . well, I don't think she is even aware of it, but there is a look in her eyes whenever she speaks of Marcus, which she does, I may say, with distressing frequency——' Her troubled green eyes lifted to her husband's. 'And I don't have to tell you where that may lead! We both know how infernally charming that brother of mine can be without his feelings ever being in the least engaged. I do think someone ought to put the child on her guard!'

'No, my dear,' said Sir Timothy with surprising firmness. 'I forbid you to interfere in this. No good ever came from meddling in other folk's affairs.'

When Sir Timothy used that tone, Hester knew better than to gainsay him. Besides, he would be none the wiser if she just dropped the odd hint in Lady Cecily's ear about Marcus's flirtations . . . the little affair of Rosanne Devine and the roses, for instance, which had come to her ears only yesterday, and before Christmas there had been an Italian opera singer forever on his arm—exquisitely beautiful, of course, but she had very soon got above herself with her jealous flights of temper.

Rumour had it he'd bought her off handsomely, but that was Marcus, amiable to the end...

'Very well,' she told Sir Timothy meekly. 'Then we must wean Lady Cecily's affections away from Marcus by less direct means. This ball will do for a start... really, I am quite in charity with him for suggesting it! A *bal masqué* might be fun, don't you think?' And with growing enthusiasm, 'Now, who do we know, dearest, who is agreeable, unwed, and immensely rich?'

Cecily returned from her outing with Mr Pendle feeling that she had worked very hard in return for the privilege of viewing the works of art at the picture gallery in Pall Mall, but determined to persevere.

She came into the Chinese room, where Lady Wigmore was resting, and sank on to the sofa with a sigh. The old lady peered at her and sniffed.

'You're not really interested in that looby, are you, Cecy?' she grunted, ever forthright.

'Mr Pendle isn't a looby, ma'am,' she protested. 'He's just a little shy.'

'Shy, is it?' Her ladyship moved impatiently in her chair. 'I've never had two coherent words out of him yet! Have you thought what it'd be like to be married to him, child? Bad enough one of you stammering, but with the two of you at it... you'll never get anything done! What?'

This last was barked out as she leaned forward, for her godchild had uttered a strangled sound, turned bright pink and finally gone off into peals of laughter.

'Whatever ails you, Cecy?' she demanded.

Cecily, who should have been mortally offended by what was, at best, a tactless observation, was instead assailed by a hilarious vision of the fate awaiting her should she succumb to Mr Pendle's charms.

'I d-don't do it... when I'm with him!' she gasped. 'Stammer, I mean... I am so busy s-setting him at ease, you see!'

'Ah!' Lady Wigmore looked discomfited. 'Yes, of course you are. Sorry, m'dear.' A rueful twinkle appeared. 'Never could mind my tongue and I'm too old to start now.'

'It doesn't matter, *truly*,' Cecily reassured her. She looked at the old lady, judged it to be a good time, and said, 'I think Mr Pendle means to invite us to the theatre. His mama is coming to town for a visit...'

'Hmph. I'll wager she's got wind that her boy's taken to mooning over you—coming to look you over, I shouldn't wonder...'

'Oh, no! I'm sure... that is...' Cecily heaved a sigh. 'Well, I dare say you may be right, ma'am. At any rate, it isn't to be a large party. Just you and me and Mrs Pendle—and Lord Sidmouth, if he can be spared from his duties at the Home Office. Lady Sidmouth is in the country at present, I believe. It was Mr Pendle's intention to ask Papa, but he, too, is out of town, so... he wondered if, perhaps, Mr Anstruther...?'

'Oh, Marcus'll stand in for him, never fear.' Lady Wigmore, recognising the inevitable and resolved to make amends for her clumsiness, was magnanimous. 'They had all better dine here first—we'll put on a fine show to impress Mr Pendle's mama.'

Oh, dear—how difficult it was! 'I rather think,' ventured Cecily, 'that Mr Pendle is intending to take the whole party to Grillon's to dine...'

'No need for him to be going to all that trouble,' declared the old lady. 'I shall tell him so when he makes his offer.'

It transpired that Mr Pendle was quite unequal to the task of standing his ground in the face of Lady Wigmore's generosity, and so the matter was decided. Cecily felt for him, though she would have wished for more resolution, and, when the time came, set herself firmly to the task of helping him through the unpredictable experience of dining with Lady Wigmore, who was liable to fire off volleys of questions from the head of the table without the least regard for the disposition of her guests or their digestions.

Mrs Pendle proved to be as thin as Lady Wigmore was gross. She had little sharp eyes which, as Lady Wigmore afterwards remarked succinctly, 'proceeded to take an inventory of m'house from the moment she entered it!'

Throughout dinner she watched as each course was impressively served under the eagle eye of Bunting, and she almost, but not quite, succeeded in out-talking her hostess.

Cecily was infinitely grateful to Mr Anstruther, who helped to smooth over the awkward moments, and conversed in such a knowledgeable way with Lord Sidmouth as to fill her with awed admiration. Almost before she knew it, the ordeal was at an end, and it was time to set out for the theatre.

Cecily had never quite accustomed herself to the clamour of town traffic, especially in the early evening, when a multitude of carriages appeared to rush about indiscriminately like wild animals, their flaming eyes stabbing the darkness before them, until it seemed that nothing less than a miracle would save them from crashing into one another.

Near the theatre the crush of vehicles was so great, the grinding and shuddering of the wheels over the cobbles so alarming, that, when these were combined with the shouts of the coachmen and postilions jostling for position and Lady Wigmore constantly banging with her stick upon the coachman's box with demands to know what was holding them up, there were times when she began to wonder if they would arrive in one piece.

But once inside, all was forgotten in the magic of the great horseshoe auditorium, which was fast filling with glittering jewelled ladies and their elegantly clad escorts. Like a child Cecily craned forward, taking a particular delight in singling out each *grande toilette*, sighing over sapphires and emeralds, and diamonds as big as pigeons' eggs. But Mr Pendle had eyes for none but Cecily; in her lavender-blue dress caught high under the brief tucked bodice with flowered streamers, and with fresh flowers in her hair, she looked what she was—a young girl hovering on the verge of womanhood, still full of innocent delight.

Finally he found the courage to stammer huskily, 'Th-there is not one among those p-painted ladies who would not give all they p-possess to change p-places with you, dear Lady Cecily.'

The others all turned to look at him, their reactions varying from outright amazement at the fervour of his declaration to kindly amusement. Cecily's blushes went unnoticed as Mr Pendle, turned bright pink, gave a nervous little cough and said defensively, 'Well, it is true!'

Above the chorus of agreement came Lady Wigmore's cackling laugh. 'So it is, young man—true enough, indeed!'

Mr Anstruther, strangely silent, was looking at Cecily intently, and not knowing what to make of the way she nibbled her lip and turned away to stare out across the auditorium. The performance was about to begin and the box directly opposite them, which had been empty, was now occupied. Two elegantly coiffured heads—one gold with that slight brassiness which owed more to art than nature, the other dark and curling at the nape—were close-joined in an attitude of intimacy; there was a glimpse of sparkling gauze, outrageously low cut... a rich, well-fitting coat. The gentleman bent closer still to murmur some remark which made the lady laugh. Something in the set of his head touched a chord in her mind, and as he sat back, she saw why—and felt sick, for the man was her father.

The sound that escaped her coincided with the rising of the curtain and was so indefinite as to pass for pleasure, but throughout the first act she was scarcely aware of what was happening onstage. Her whole attention was riveted on the box opposite, until at last she drew Papa's laughing eyes to hers, saw them go blank with shock, watched unblinking as belongings were hurriedly caught up, a fur-trimmed wrap flung about the lady's shoulders, and then the box was empty again.

As far as Cecily could tell, she was the only one to have noticed anything amiss. For the remainder of the evening she made a determined effort to behave normally, saying all the right things to Mr Pendle when required to do so and avoiding all the while Mr Anstruther's too-penetrating gaze. Upon arriving back in Portland Place, Lady Wigmore pronounced it to have been a most satisfactory evening...she had not dozed off above twice during the whole performance and *that young man* had behaved exactly as he ought, though she didn't think much of the mother...

At last Cecily was free to go to her bed, but she passed a wretched night, her dreams uninvaded by Mr Pendle or his mama, for every time she closed her eyes her mind was filled with the memory of the golden-haired lady smiling up at Papa in that quite unmistakable way. She was no longer naïve—one could not be long in London, after all, without discovering that even the most respectable of gentlemen sometimes kept mistresses, and though deeply shocked at first she had been able to quiet her sensibilities with the reflection that London manners must render acceptable much that would be frowned upon at home. It had simply never occurred to her that Papa might be one of their number, and yet now she knew it seemed incredible that she had not guessed sooner!

Every instinct urged that pity for Mama must supersede all else, but morning found her still wrestling with her conscience. Papa had long ceased to figure in her mind as the gay handsome gentleman with the twinkling eyes whose infrequent visits home had set the whole place in a buzz of laughter and activity, with Mama looking happy and bringing out all her prettiest dresses and lots of balls and parties! *That* image had tarnished even before Cecily had been obliged, too soon, to relieve her ailing mother of the household reins: it was to vanish completely with the discovery that there was frequently no money to pay the staff or the tradesmen's bills and that after one of Papa's periodic repairing leases what few resources remained were usually sadly depleted. Yet, though she knew him to be feckless, he was a charmer still and she forgave him much—more than Bella did—and in these last few weeks she had felt much closer to him than ever before.

She dressed in a mood of abstraction that had Lizzie in a positive ferment of curiosity after the events of the previous evening, while Bunting was much concerned to learn that their young guest, whom Cook had so often commended for the excellence of her appetite, had made such a poor breakfast. Over-excitement, belike. Nor did Lady Cecily seem much cheered when he informed her later in the morning that Lord Camden had called and was awaiting her in the front drawing-room.

Cecily found her father staring out of the window. He appeared not to have heard the door and she was halfway across the room before he turned. The bright morning light was merciless, highlighting in a way she had not noticed, or wished to notice before, the ravages that dissipation was carving into the still-handsome features. In one cheek a nerve twitched spasmodically.

'Cecy!' He came towards her, arms outstretched, falsely jovial like a small boy trying to brazen his way out of a misdemeanour. 'Dear Cecy! I still can't believe that you are eighteen! You look exactly as you did when I used to swing you up on my shoulder! Do you remember?'

Oh, that was unfair! She stiffened, enduring his embrace, but not returning it. Just for an instant he rested his cheek against hers and murmured her name again, only this time it was more in the nature of a desperate plea for understanding. Her throat ached abominably; she wanted to respond, but not here, not now, when they were liable to be interrupted at any moment.

As if induced by thought, there was a sound beyond the door and he released her just as it opened to admit Lady Wigmore, followed closely by her nephew, with whom she appeared to be locked in verbal combat. Cecily was shocked out of her own troubles by the sight of her godmother leaning heavily upon a stout stick. As the old lady propelled her immense bulk across the room with obvious discomfort, she ran to help her.

'Let me be, child—don't fuss!' she panted, sinking into her chair amid clouds of grey crêpe. 'Lord, first it's Marcus and now you! And all over nothing more than a gouty knee that plagues me from time to time! Twisted it getting out of m'bed. Nothing to be done about it.'

Cecily's worried glance went winging to Mr Anstruther, who only raised an eyebrow and said without heat, 'You might, of course, try paying heed to Dr Marston.'

'That prying, sententious old windbag! Small use he is to anyone with his megrims and his pettyfogging notions! Always preaching abstinence and muttering on about beneficial diets and taking the waters. The man should have been a parson. He'd take a positive delight in showing people the error of their ways!'

Her nephew shrugged in amused resignation and, having seen her safely bestowed in her chair, went to lounge elegantly against the fireplace, one hand idly fingering a small black marble urn, one of several adorning the mantelshelf, as he pondered on the curious atmosphere existing between father and daughter.

Lady Wigmore, less than usually observant, said brusquely, 'Well—good morning to you, Camden. I hope I see you well?' She brushed aside his charmingly uttered commiserations upon her injury and his hopes that it wasn't paining her too greatly. ''Tis a nuisance, sir—no more! Pity you were out of town last night. Cecy's beau took us to the theatre—very keen to have you along. But there!' A rumble of mirth shook her. 'Brought his mama—dreadful encroaching female! Very interesting! I expect Cecy has been telling you all about it, eh?'

Cecily glanced at her papa in mute appeal and then, very much aware of Mr Anstruther's interest, stammered that he had arrived but a few minutes since and wished to take her for a drive. The earl, rising nobly to the occasion, backed her up.

'Well, Cecy,' said Mr Anstruther whimsically, 'it seems we have both come on the same errand. I concede, however, that your father must have the prior claim.'

Her smile was a poor effort.

'Vastly obliging of you, Marcus,' said Lady Wigmore. 'Run along, then, child and put on your bonnet. You'll not forget we are dining with the Seftons?'

'Oh, but . . . should we not cancel? Your leg . . . ?'

'My leg ain't going to rule my life. It hasn't done so in the past and I don't aim to let it start now!'

The earl said heartily, 'I'll have Cecy back in good time, never fear.'

Mr Anstruther walked across to open the door for Cecily, subjecting her as he did so to a searching look. 'Do you wish to go?' he asked quietly.

'Yes, of course I do,' she said, hurrying away before he could ask awkward questions. But it was not to be that simple. Her name was called imperatively and she turned to find that he had followed her. She stood, irresolute, as he came close and placed one slim finger under her chin, raising it gently; felt herself colouring under the acuteness of those sleepy eyes.

'Then don't look so troubled,' he said, shaking his head at her. 'And be advised, my dear—don't think too harshly of your father!'

Cecily looked startled. 'You saw them also? Last night, I m-mean?'

'Yes, of course,' he said calmly. 'But I'm sorry that *you* did, though there was always the chance that it would happen some time, I suppose.'

'You knew! I expect everyone knows but me! You might have w-warned me!'

Wry amusement lit his eyes. 'My dear girl, it is hardly the easiest of tasks, to impart an intelligence of so delicate a nature to an innocent young girl, especially when it most concerns her father!'

Cecily drew back, stiffening. 'Of course not! I dare say it might offend one of your stupid codes of honour!' she accused him angrily. 'Gentlemen! You put me out of all patience! I am not *that* innocent!' Before he had recovered sufficiently to answer, she swept away and left him.

There were very few people about as her father guided his smart little chaise through the quiet streets. He seemed loath to open the conversation, and Cecily, still smarting with shame over her outburst against Mr Anstruther, was equally diffident. But the time came when she could bear the silence no longer.

'Papa... could we please t-talk?' she pleaded.

He brought the chaise to a halt and sat pleating the reins back and forth through his fingers. Her own hands were clasped tight in her lap.

'I'm not sure I know what to say to you, Cecy. Perhaps I would have been better advised not to come...'

'Oh, no!'

'. . . except that I couldn't live with the memory of that look in your eyes last night.' He patted her hands without looking at her. 'You have always been my conscience, d'you know that? More than your mother, even, I've always minded what you thought! I can see you now, my little dreamer with the practical soul, endeavouring to explain to me with a gravity way beyond your years about rents and wages—all those mundane facts of life I declined to concern myself with—such as how difficult it was to keep Churston going——'

'I never m-meant to be critical,' she said in a stifled voice.

'But you weren't, that was the miraculous thing!' The hand patting hers gripped them tightly and his own voice was gruff. 'Your mother and Bella complained, yet you saw me so clearly and never judged me once. That's why, when it was decided that you should come to London, I was so scared . . .'

'Scared? You?'

'Out of my life!' he said wryly. 'Now at last, I told myself, she will see what you're *really* like—the depths to which you have sunk! But I have tried—since that first night when I almost ruined things for you—I really have tried to be discreet. Last night was just a terrible blunder. Dolly had been out of town, d'you see? Last evening I brought her back and we decided to celebrate with a visit to the theatre.'

'How long have you...?' Cecily stammered. She was unable to finish, but her meaning was plain.

'Oh, Dolly is just one in a long line,' he said harshly. 'No, that isn't fair—she has lasted rather longer than most and puts up with my humours far more patiently than I deserve!' The earl stopped and then said violently, 'Dammit, I shouldn't be talking to you like this!'

'Oh, please!' she insisted resolutely. 'You see, I very much w-want to understand.'

He laughed, almost in despair. 'Oh, my dearest Cecy! You, of all people, could never understand...and I don't want you to!' He took her hands and made her look at him. 'Listen to me, my dear. For once I intend to be quite unselfish. I want you to forget about my troubles...'

'But...'

'No buts. I dare say you have visions of marrying someone very rich who will settle my debts. Well, perhaps I once had the same vision—I expect you'll have guessed that Jack Elliston is more than keen to offer for you.' She made a distressed sound and he hurried on, 'Have no fear, puss, in a moment of madness I might have considered the possibility, but I had only to see him in your company to realise how unthinkable such a match would be!' With sudden vehemence, he added, 'In fact, I wouldn't let him lay a finger on you. No matter what the cost!'

Relief flooded through her, yet she was moved to venture with diffidence, 'But you do owe Mr Elliston a lot of money?'

'You are not to worry your pretty little head about that, puss!' The earl's smile was peculiarly sweet. 'I've been at point nonplus before now and have come about. No. I want you to find yourself a man if you can who will care for you, one whom you can marry for your own heart's sake or even for the sake of your mama and the girls if you must, but not, I beg of you, from any idiotish notion of saving me from the consequences of my crass folly! That only time and my own wits can resolve.'

CHAPTER SIX

SHEER force of will carried Lady Wigmore through their dinner with the Seftons, but the following morning she was confined to her room, the knee being much inflamed by her unwise exertions. No amount of entreaty, however, by those closest to her could persuade her to summon Dr Marston. Nor would she stay in her bed, in spite of a sleepless night which had left her more than usually crabby.

'I'll take to my bed when I want to sleep or die—and I ain't figuring on doing either right now!' she declared through gritted teeth as three sturdy footmen and her personal maid, Picton, heaved and manhandled her into a chair where Cecily waited to wrap her around with a rug. 'And I'll not have Marcus up here browbeating me, either!' The improbability of Mr Anstruther's browbeating anyone made Cecily smile. 'A-ha! You think him incapable of it just because he don't raise his voice! Well, let me tell you, child—that smooth-tongued charm of his'd wear down the devil himself, so you just keep him away from me!'

With no very clear idea of how this was to be accomplished if he decided otherwise, Cecily awaited Mr Anstruther's arrival in some trepidation, very much aware that her behaviour of the previous day must place her at a disadvantage. But when he came at last, he made the whole thing easy by owning most charmingly that the fault had been his for presuming to tell her how to go on with her own father. By the time she had finished assuring him that it had been nothing of the kind, that she had come to a much greater measure of understanding with her father, and that she was more than grateful for his continuing interest, they were once more on amiable terms and she was able to answer his queries about Lady Wigmore with tolerable composure.

'You needn't try so hard to be tactful, infant,' he assured her. 'Bunting has explained all with his usual aplomb. I shall let matters lie for the present, but be warned—Aunt Constance can be an abominably unreasonable patient and I don't mean to let her wear you out!'

Cecily assured him that there was not the least likelihood of this . . . if only she might in some way repay her godmother's kindness.

'Do you think Lady Wigmore might be amenable to having some very particular herbal fomentations applied to her poor knee? We had great success with them last winter when Cook suffered a severe inflammation of the knee.'

Mr Anstruther had a pretty fair idea of what his aunt's reaction would be, but it was a serious question and he answered with perfect gravity, avowing that fomentations sounded the very thing and that his aunt would prove herself to be the most shockingly ungrateful creature alive an' she rejected them.

'But I am prepared to countenance these charitable ministrations only if I have your assurance that they will in no way curtail your engagements.'

'Oh, pooh!' she declared. 'It would be a tragedy indeed if I should be obliged to forgo a few paltry parties!'

'Paltry!' Mr Anstruther looked deeply shocked. 'My dear young lady, you will never achieve your ambition if this is to be your attitude!'

The absurdity drew from her a gurgle of laughter, the more so as he protested, 'I am serious, madam! If your own reputation means so little to you, then I beg you will consider mine!' He waggled his quizzing glass reprovingly under her nose. 'I have been at great pains to present you to the world as an aspiring young lady of fashion—and young ladies of fashion, my dear, do not have so little regard for the delights of society that they prefer to stay at home applying fomentations, which task might quite properly be delegated to some menial better qualified for it—that frosty-faced maid, Picton, for instance.'

'Oh, no!' It was Cecily's turn to feign shock. 'Picton would deem such an undertaking very much beneath her dignity! And besides,' she continued more seriously, 'I should prefer to attend to Lady

Wigmore myself, for I very much fear she may have tired herself through overtaxing her energies on my behalf.'

Mr Anstruther's eyes warmed as he looked down at her. 'If she has, only consider that neither of us could have stopped her. You have brought her a great deal of pleasure, you know, and the last thing she would want is for you to withdraw from any of the engagements she had planned for you.' He frowned. 'Are you not to make your debut at Almack's tonight?'

'Yes. Lady Wigmore had thought perhaps your sister...but Lady Sefton has very kindly offered to chaperon me...'

'The deuce she has!' Mr Anstruther's eyebrow described a gentle arch. 'You are fortunate, indeed, to make your first appearance under the aegis of one of the patronesses!'

'Shall you be there?' Cecily asked shyly.

'Oh, you won't need me! With so august a sponsor as Lady Sefton, you won't want for partners.'

'Perhaps not,' she said doubtfully. 'But that is not the same as having one's friends, is it?'

He let the quizzing glass fall and possessed himself of one of her hands. 'Is that how you regard me?' he said, smiling faintly. 'I am honoured.'

'You don't think me presumptuous?'

'Not in the least.' His smile deepened. He said, not having meant to at all, 'Shall we drive in the park this afternoon if you are not engaged elsewhere? We haven't done so for several days.'

'Oh, but I didn't m-mean...' She broke off, swallowed and drew a steadying breath. If only he wouldn't look at her in quite that way. It was very difficult to remember that he was only being kind. 'I w-wouldn't have you think...that is, you mustn't feel yourself under the least obligation...'

'I don't,' he said, enjoying himself enormously. 'Dear Lady Cecily, are you aware that you blush quite delightfully when you are lost in confusion?'

'Yes, sir. It is a sore trial to me. But *you* are really not playing fair,' she pointed out reproachfully, 'for you are still holding my hand!'

'So I am. Such a pretty member it is, too.' He regarded it a moment, lifted it lightly to his lips, and released it. Cecily came out of a slight daze to hear him say in his old teasing way, 'Well, madam, do you accept my invitation? Come, you need not fear that I shall make a scene if you refuse. I hope I shall accept my *congé* like a gentleman!'

It was not difficult after all to respond in similar vein, to say with rather more than her usual spirit, 'Thank you, sir. Yes, of course I will accept. Eliza says that it adds greatly to my consequence to be seen in your company...indeed, you t-told me as much yourself!' And as this received a decidedly quizzical look, 'At least, I dare say you didn't phrase it in quite that way, but it was what you meant!'

'Was it? Well, it may have been true once, but I think you will not have need of my support for much longer.'

When Mr Anstruther arrived at Almack's Assembly Rooms almost midway through the evening, it appeared that he had already been proved right. Cecily, he was told by a delighted Eliza, had scarcely been off her feet throughout the whole evening.

'Quite a small triumph, in fact. She has danced the cotillion with Lord Palmerston and been complimented by George Brummell, who looked in for a short while with Cecy's father. *And* she has annoyed the baroness quite excessively by capturing the interest of her son! This is the second country dance he has bespoken... I rather wondered that Lady Sefton should permit it. I know poor Cecy was hoping very much that she wouldn't!' Eliza sighed. 'I really believe I have never seen her look better.'

It was true, he thought, discovering in himself something of the pride of possession. In her pale-blue ballgown with the silver embroidery, one of the first they had bought, and with her smoky fair curls confined in a ribbon, she appeared to float rather than dance, an illusion enhanced by the heavy unyielding figure of her partner.

On the far side of the room the Baroness von Oppenheimer sat with Princess Esterhazy, whose fan wafted lazily back and forth as her companion made disparaging comments about young people who flaunted themselves unbecomingly in public, eyes narrowing as they rested on the ethereal young figure at present hand in hand with her Frederick.

'The girl with the parasol, they are calling her, did you know? Such a pity that Lady Wigmore has persuaded her nephew to single the girl out—though of course we all know why! The family is impoverished and she must needs redress the balance. But as a consequence of his attentions that insignificant child is given ideas that are quite beyond her! I notice Mr Anstruther is showing little sign of offering for her himself!' Her laugh was a trifle shrill.

'Perhaps not, but one can hardly term the daughter of an earl, however impoverished, insignificant, I think?' The wife of the Austrian ambassador was deriving a certain malicious amusement from her companion's discomfiture.

Cecily was feeling a little discomfited herself; at that precise moment she was fully occupied in trying to prevent the baron's odious attentions from exceeding the bounds of civility, and was obliged to keep in the forefront of her mind the various strictures lovingly instilled by Miss Gilbert concerning politeness to others!

It was several minutes before she became aware of Mr Anstruther, superbly elegant in the knee breeches and silk stockings that were *de rigueur* for all gentlemen attending Almack's. He was quite the most handsome man present, she reflected with partiality, so lost in contemplation of his superior qualities that she missed her step and found her toes crushed beneath the baron's less-than-nimble feet.

But mercifully the set was drawing to a close; she was able to shut her ears to the fulsome compliments, thank him politely, and seat herself demurely at Lady Sefton's side to await Mr Anstruther. It seemed an age before he came, and another age as he conversed with Lady Sefton, saying everything that was proper while his eyes, catching hers, danced most improperly. Finally he led her out on to the floor.

'I was beginning to wonder if you would come,' she confessed. 'You never actually said you would.'

'How could I stay away on such an occasion?' he murmured, teasing. 'Although now the Beau has approved you, you will have no time for me!'

'That is very silly,' she reproved him. 'Mr Brummell is certainly very fine, but I didn't like him half as well as you.'

Mr Anstruther's eyes laughed at her as they moved down the dance. 'That is an encomium which any gentleman must treasure!'

Happiness bubbled precariously in her throat. 'I w-wanted to thank you for your lovely flowers,' she said shyly, touching the posy at her bosom. 'I have never been given flowers before.'

'Well, you will be given lots in the future. I'm glad that mine are the first.' They were separated by the dance, and when they came together again, he looked around. 'No Mr Pendle this evening?'

'He could not obtain vouchers in time.' An irrepressible giggle escaped her. 'His mama was furious!'

'Heartless girl!'

'Oh, I know one shouldn't laugh and indeed I do not dislike *Mr* Pendle.'

Mr Anstruther readily agreed that it was Mrs Pendle who stuck like a bone in the throat, but prophesied that by the end of this evening Cecily's choice of suitors should have widened considerably. The prospect ought to have cheered her, but instead left her with a curious flat feeling which she attempted to dispel with the reflection that at least she was in no danger of receiving an offer from Mr Elliston... her papa had given her a positive assurance upon that head. Mr Anstruther wondered whether the earl had been as frank with Mr Elliston, but he did not voice his doubts aloud, setting himself instead to charming her back into humour.

Lady Hester, watching them together, was furious with her brother. How could a man of his experience not be aware of the effect he was having upon Lady Cecily when her heart was shining out of her eyes for all to see? Something must be done!

The very next morning she arrived in Portland Place, having astonished her household by rising well before her usual hour so that she might be in advance of any purely social callers. She swept past the porter on the door, a vision in bronze-green twilled silk with an outrageously stylish chip hat tied with a flourish just beneath one ear, and announced to a somewhat bemused Bunting that she was come to enquire after her aunt. He informed her that her ladyship had passed a tolerably comfortable night, but he rather thought a visit so early in the day might be unwise.

Hester was quick to agree that it would be most unwise, but rather thought that now she was here she might just look in on Lady Cecily. The butler's voice took on a kindly note as he told her that Lady Cecily had been about bright and early and could probably be found in the music-room, where she had formed the habit of passing the early part of the morning.

'Good. Then I will go on up. No, you need not go with me—I am sure we need not stand on ceremony!' She lifted a languid hand and bestowed upon him a smile so reminiscent of her brother in his younger days as to arouse in Bunting the unworthy suspicion that the young lady was up to something!

Hester, meanwhile, was scratching upon the music-room door and begging that Cecily would tell her at once if she was disturbing the muse.

'No, indeed! Do pray come in!'

Hester stripped off her gloves and tossed them carelessly on to a table together with her reticule before draping herself elegantly upon the nearest sofa. Cecily reseated herself at the spinet, turning a little aside with her hands clasped around her knee as she chattered on happily about the previous evening and how she hadn't found Almack's half so tedious as Mr Anstruther had led her to expect. Hester reflected that she looked little more than a child with her undressed hair tumbling almost to her shoulders. And yet there was something disturbingly new and not in the least childlike about her—a growing awareness, a kind of bloom which had not been there before.

Such a pity to blight that shining happiness before it had even a chance to come to fruition, sighed Hester, but better a little hurt now than heartbreak later. She brought the conversation around to her proposed *bal masqué*, now only days away.

'Is your dress decided upon?'

'We thought perhaps a French court dress of the Louis Quinze period?' Cecily nibbled her lip, remembering with guilt the expense. '*À la Watteau*, you know.'

Hester didn't ask to whom the 'we' referred. 'The very thing, my dear!' she exclaimed. 'You will look quite delightful, and with that pretty hair skilfully dressed you won't need to wear a wig!' And then, casually, 'Does my brother come as Louis?'

'Oh, I think not!' Cecily's dimples showed. 'I don't see Mr Anstruther in costume, somehow, do you?'

'Not unless Weston could be persuaded to design it!' said his sister drily. 'Still, that is no reason for the rest of us to be so poor-spirited. I intend to allow my fancy free rein. I have cast Sir Timothy as a cavalier, while for myself I favour something along classical Grecian lines. You know I am vastly indebted to Marcus! Only fancy, I was so reluctant when he first coaxed me into holding the ball—though it was not at that time to be a masquerade, of course!'

'Mr Anstruther asked you to hold the ball?'

'Why, yes! Did he not tell you? Oh, dear!' Hester made an artless little moue. 'I had not supposed there to be any secret about it! Perhaps you had better not mention that I have told you...for someone who is by nature the most amiable of creatures, he can grow decidedly miffy if he feels one has betrayed a confidence!'

'Of course I will say nothing if that is what you wish, but I don't see...'

'The thing is, you see, that Marcus conceived the whole thing for your benefit! He has really grown quite fond of you, so that what began as a favour to Aunt Constance has now grown into a sincere determination to see you well married. Truly, I have seldom known him to be quite so single minded—except, of course, when he fancies himself in love.

Then, no extravagance is spared!' Hester heard the sharp indrawing of breath and was obliged to remind herself that what she was doing was for Cecily's own good. She hurried on, 'Life for Marcus is an amusing game, a continuing challenge to his skills, whether it be a matter of flooring the great Jackson with a punishing left, or pursuing Madame Devine with pink roses—just think of it, my dear, fresh roses every day, delivered from his own hothouses in the country—and all for love! Could anything be more romantic—or more ridiculous? And then you present a new challenge to his ingenuity and *madame* is forgotten!'

Cecily's head was bent, her voice muffled. 'You make him sound shallow—and quite horrid!'

'Good gracious! Nothing of the kind!' Hester realised that she had gone too far in her bid to discourage the younger girl. 'I am devoted to Marcus, so kind as he is—truly charming, and generous to a fault, just so long as one doesn't take him too seriously.' She felt like a murderer, but whatever she had been expecting it was not the quiet composed face that Cecily finally lifted to her; apart from a slight blankness in her eyes there was nothing remarkable in the polite gravity of her 'Yes, I see. Thank you.'

Hester wasn't sure what she was being thanked for, and as the clock chimed at that moment she seized the opportunity to cry with a shriek of dismay, 'Heavens! Is that the time? My dear child,

I must fly!' and rose with something less than her usual grace, collected up her belongings, and exhorting her to come soon and see the children, who were always asking after her, she dropped a light kiss on Cecily's cheek and was gone in a rustling of silk.

CHAPTER SEVEN

CECILY sat for a long time after Hester had gone before going quietly up to her room. Mr Anstruther's flowers had been given pride of place on the dresser. The edges of the posy's outer petals were beginning to curl slightly, but otherwise it was surprisingly fresh. She lifted it from its jug of water and carried it to her favourite window seat, heedless of the water dripping down on to her dress. And there she sat with her nose buried in the bittersweet fragrance of violets and jonquils—fresh springtime blooms with not a hot-house rose among them! How Bella would scoff if she could see her now—poor foolish Cecy, day-dreaming again—and she would be right, for that was all it amounted to: foolish dreams. Just for a little while, in her innocence, she had invested the posy with a significance beyond its merit, not knowing how liberally Mr Anstruther bestowed his floral tributes. Looking back, she could even remember his wearing a pink rose in his lapel at their first meeting, a tribute to the unknown Madame Devine!

She must be grateful to Hester for putting his gift to her in perspective—as a generous offering to someone whom he regarded with a certain indulgence, to make her feel important. Tears of regret rained down briefly on the wilting petals and then resolutely she placed the posy back in its jug, blew her nose, washed her face, and went along to attend to Lady Wigmore's knee.

To the surprise of all concerned, Lady Wigmore had offered no more than a token resistance to Cecily's suggested treatment. In point of fact, the knee had quickly become so confoundedly swollen and painful that, underneath her outward thunderous defiance, there lurked a very real, unspoken dread that she might dwindle into a helpless old woman dependent on others and despised by them. Already she could sense an air of pessimism, shared by all, it seemed, except this gel, of whom she had grown so fond and whose candid concern found expression in an earnest desire to help.

No one, least of all her ladyship, entertained any real hope that Lady Cecily's odd, homespun remedies were capable of alleviating so severe a condition, but only Picton was overtly disapproving. In her opinion Dr Marston should have been summoned immediately. She could not think it seemly that any gently nurtured young lady should feel herself able to view a limb grown so grotesque as her ladyship's without having instant recourse to the hartshorn, let alone take herself off to the kitchens in order to supervise the mixing of poultices! That she could then bring herself to apply the same to Lady Wigmore's leg with her own hands and without the least semblance of distaste, morning, noon and evening, no matter what pleasures might have to wait upon her labours, displayed, to Picton's way of thinking, a want of sensibility quite unacceptable in an earl's daughter.

Cecily felt the weight of Picton's displeasure, but steeled herself to ignore it. She believed she would have done so even if she had not already glimpsed the helpless fear in the old lady's eyes; as it was, she was determined to persevere. After three days she was rewarded by a very definite improvement, and at the end of a week Lady Wigmore was able to bear her weight sufficiently well to hobble with help as far as the Chinese room. She did not find it easy to express her gratitude in words and Cecily begged that she would not try.

'Well, I'll not have you forgoing any more outings on my account, d'you hear me now?' The old lady pointed an accusing forefinger at her. 'You thought you could bamboozle me, I dare say, but I had Mrs Longford here this morning and she said you was expected at a Venetian breakfast out at Chiswick two days since and you cried off! What do you say to that, miss? Eh?'

'I didn't particularly wish to go, ma'am.'

'Didn't you, now? And how many other functions have you not wished to go to, I wonder?'

'Not *very* many,' said Cecily, incurably truthful. 'None that I cared about greatly, at any rate. So many parties can be very tiring, you know, when one is not accustomed to them. I have been quite glad of the chance to stay at home occasionally.'

'Oh, Cecy, my dear child!' Lady Wigmore reached out an unsteady hand, and those who thought they knew her would have been astonished to observe an unfamiliar softness in her eyes. 'You did not come to London in order to stay quietly at home! I have not done very well by you, I fear.'

Cecily grasped the hand in both of hers, reassuringly. 'That is nonsensical and you know it! I am having a perfectly splendid time. A few days can hardly signify.'

'The fact remains that you're looking decidedly peaky. Why, at your age I could dance every night away and still have energy enough for breakfasts and picnics and goodness knows what else besides! There is Bunting telling me of Mr Pendle forever on the doorstep, not to mention Bayldon and young Widdlesham. *And* I suspect many of those flowers which somehow found their way to my room were intended for quite another purpose! You should be seizing your opportunities, gel!'

Mention of flowers inevitably brought thoughts of Mr Anstruther. He had been summoned by his father, who had been unwell for some time and wished to consult Mr Anstruther on a matter of business. Soon after Hester's visit he had called briefly in Portland Place but had been too preoccupied to notice anything amiss in Cecily's behaviour towards him. She was sorry about his father, but the break had been fortuitous, allowing her time to come to terms with herself. His flowers, now faded, had been pressed into a favourite book of poetry along with her dreams, and she felt sure that when he returned she would be able to face him with complete equanimity.

'A pity Marcus had to go away when he did,' said the old lady as though reading her thoughts. 'He wouldn't have swallowed all that humgudgeon you think to serve up to me—he wouldn't have allowed you to get so moped, either!'

'I protest ma'am!' cried Cecily between laughing and indignation. 'What a very unflattering picture you paint of me. My days have certainly been a little curtailed, but I have scarcely been above a night at home! Eliza and Harry have made sure of that. And now that you are so much improved, I hope you will have no further cause for complaint in me. Indeed,' she added reassuringly, 'I am so much in demand over the next few days that I shall be lucky if I see my bed at all! But I must have your assurance that you will not overtax yourself and undo all my good work.'

'Oh, you must, must you?' Lady Wigmore sniffed and did her utmost to look fierce. 'Oh, very well!' She cackled suddenly. 'At least I shall miss that masquerade nonsense of Hester's. Tomorrow night, is it not? I'd hoped to see Marcus back by then.'

She did not notice the delicate flush staining Cecily's cheek.

'Mr Anstruther did p-promise that he would return in time,' Cecily said, and was pleased at the ease with which his name came out.

Lady Wigmore presently fell into a gentle doze and began to snore. Cecily slipped quietly out of the room and was promptly met by Bunting, who presented her with the Baron von Oppenheimer's card, his expression conveying more graphically than words his opinion of that gentleman.

The baron wished to take her for a drive. Did his mother know? Cecily wondered. She hesitated, searching for the words to refuse him without giving offence. It was at such times that she envied Eliza her ease of manner.

'I d-don't think . . . my godmother . . .' she began inadequately.

He was all pomp, lifting slightly on the balls of his feet in an assured, considering way. 'There can be no objection, dear Lady Cecily. Open carriage, you know—groom in attendance—all perfectly proper, I assure you. Lady Wigmore may be quite at ease upon that head!'

Cecily decided that it would be easier to concede defeat than to argue. With any luck he would be driving that pair of spirited greys he had bragged of buying, the ones Harry had prophesied with fiendish glee that he would have the devil's own job to hold. If so, at least she need not fear to be pawed!

The park was reached without any incident more serious than the baron's managing to scrape the wheels of his chaise along one side of a closed carriage upon turning a corner too sharply, a piece of carelessness which brought down upon him a stream of invective from the occupant of the carriage. The worst Cecily had to endure was a long and boring dissertation upon his recent visit to Italy, interspersed with the occasional lascivious glance and some overly civil comments upon her appearance which brought a little angry colour stealing into her face.

Once in the park, however, they soon came upon Mr Pendle, who glared at the baron with ill-concealed jealousy and insisted upon riding alongside them the whole length of the tan. To Cecily his presence brought a welcome relief, but the baron was so incensed that he grew careless with the reins and the greys, still fresh, got away from him and became entangled in an oncoming barouche.

In the midst of the resulting confusion Harry Ireland came upon the scene driving his own gig. Mr Pendle had already dismounted and was helping Cecily down from the chaise while the baron's groom and two other gentlemen strove to contain the horses. Harry watched with growing delight as Mr Pendle fussed over Cecily, assuring himself that she was uninjured before rushing to rescue her parasol, which was now bobbing gently about on the grass.

When all this had been accomplished, Harry brought his gig up and hailed them in the unflurried manner of one accustomed to commanding order out of chaos. 'My dear Lady Cecily! This seems a most ill-managed business. You must permit me to take you home at once. I shall own myself surprised if the experience does not result in a severe shock to the nerves!'

The solemnity of this declaration was enough to betray his humour to Cecily and, without daring to look him in the eye, she allowed a disappointed Mr Pendle to assist her into the gig, expressing as he did so his earnest aspirations that she would be well enough to visit Vauxhall that evening. The gig moved away and their last sight was of the occupant of the barouche descending to do battle, and of the baron's portly figure jumping up and down with rage as he berated the poor grooms valiantly striving to untangle the horses amid a gathering crowd of amused spectators.

It was all that Cecily could do to restrain her mirth until they were out of earshot; then, one look into Harry's brimming eyes and she fell to giggling.

'The p-poor baron!'

'Poor, my eye! Oh, just wait until I tell Eliza!' Harry gasped, wiping his eyes. 'She'll never believe it! My dear Cecy, however did you come to be in the company of that egregious ass?'

'He was so very p-pressing, you see! And I could not get him to go away!'

'Well, I shouldn't think you'll be troubled again! I doubt the gentleman's ardour will survive the ridicule this afternoon's débâcle must heap upon him! And if *he* forgives you, his mother never will!'

'Well, I'm very sorry for the baron,' Cecily owned frankly, 'but I don't see that I can be held accountable for his bad temper, or the fact that he has a shocking pair of hands! As for his mother, she must do as she pleases!'

Mr Pendle, much moved by her near escape from mortal danger, proposed at Vauxhall that same evening, made bold by the idyllic nature of his surroundings; the sylvan glades brilliantly illuminated with coloured lamps and the sounds of music wafting on the air. At least Cecily, who had never been proposed to before, took the incoherent protestations of devotion, the hope that she might permit him to approach her father, to amount to a proposal.

Until that moment it had been a most enjoyable evening. They had drunk champagne and partaken of wafer-thin slivers of ham and baby chicks in one of the supper boxes surrounding the Grove. They had listened to the musicians and Cecily, for whom such things were still sufficient of a novelty, had exclaimed pleasurably over the entertainments provided, the fireworks in all their splendour, the tumblers and singers and jugglers.

Champagne was magnificently clearing to the brain, she confided to Eliza, adding suddenly with all the confidence of this newfound lucidity, 'You and Harry should be married. Why are you not, when you are plainly made for one another?'

Eliza chuckled. 'Because he hasn't asked me, my love. I think he has reservations about impoverished officers on half-pay and with few prospects marrying wealthy young women.'

'Oh, but that is absurd!'

'It may seem so to you and I, Cecy, but gentlemen can be very sensitive about such things.'

'Yes, I suppose so. Somehow I had never thought of you as being wealthy.' Cecily added with a wistful sigh, 'It must be very agreeable.'

Eliza's smile was rueful. 'Well, of course, it would be hypocritical of me to deny the advantages of being a rich man's daughter, but there are times when it can become a confounded bore.'

Cecily found this very hard to believe. 'I think you would make a splendid soldier's wife and would like nothing better than to follow the drum. I shall tell Harry so!'

'No, no, I beg of you!' Eliza pleaded. 'Of course I mean to have Harry, but I would as lief you let me approach it in my own way!'

'Very well,' Cecily agreed magnanimously.

Now that she was faced with Mr Pendle's flushed eagerness, it came upon her with equal clarity how the light from the hundreds of lanterns accentuated the youthful indecision prevailing in his features. Even his amiability, though admirable in its way, lacked the kind of assertiveness which must encourage one to repose one's confidence in him. Cecily supposed the fault lay in his upbringing, but she was disappointed that he had not improved upon acquaintance as much as she had hoped. She stifled an unreasoning urge to compare him with that certain other gentleman, in whom could be found all the virtues one might wish for in a husband, and begged that he would allow her a little while for reflection—though common sense informed her that she might well do worse. After all, the very malleability of Mr Pendle's temperament could be turned to advantage, for though Papa had begged that she would not regard his need there was little doubt in her mind that she might, with the greatest ease, persuade Mr Pendle to settle at least some of Papa's debts. It was a consideration not to be ignored, greatly though it depressed her.

She came home that night ready to fall into her bed, so that when the twist of paper dropped from her reticule she almost let it lie; simple curiosity in the end obliged her to investigate it further. It was a note, addressed to her in the painstaking hand of someone seldom called upon to put pen to paper. Her eyes skimmed over the words, and then she was smoothing out the paper, moving closer to the light to read it again with growing disquiet and puzzlement. Certain phrases stood out...'sorely concerned about the earl, your father...against his wishes...beg you to meet me...' and at the end, heavily underscored, 'Do not fail me!' It was sighed, 'y'r obedient servant, Dolly Preston'.

Cecily did not know what to make of it, but vowed that she would be at the Stanhope Gate on the stroke of nine o'clock as the note besought her. She lay awake, jolted out of her tiredness, poor Mr Pendle once more relegated to a position of little importance at the back of her mind, and fretted over what could have prompted her father's mistress to write with such apparent desperation.

Lizzie, creeping into the room on the following morning in the confident expectation of hearing her mistress still gently snoring, found her already up and dressed for riding. Taken aback, Lizzie was betrayed into blurting out that milady was never going out at this hour of a morning!

'Not immediately.' Cecily, too preoccupied to recognise any impertinence, was busily engaged in setting a neat little riding hat with unintentional pertness over her eyes. She picked up her gloves and crop. 'In fact, I believe I might manage a cup of coffee before I leave if you would be so kind as to run down and ask Cook. Tell her I will take breakfast when I return...' she thought quickly '...in about an hour, I should think.'

Bunting, too, looked vaguely disapproving when he was presently required to arrange that a horse be saddled for her. Cecily gave him her most persuasive smile.

'Surely it is not so very dreadful to wish to take a ride before breakfast? Quite a short ride—as far as the park and back?'

Thus put on the spot, the butler was obliged to acknowledge that if Lady Cecily were to take a groom—as he was sure she meant to—there could be no real objection, though her ladyship would most likely disapprove if she came to know.

Cecily wrinkled her nose at him. 'Then we won't tell her, will we?' she coaxed.

Bunting's mouth was still prim, but there was suddenly a great deal of comprehension in his eyes. He only knew of one cause that would take a normally sensible young miss such as Lady Cecily gallivanting out before her breakfast on a morning that was like to become inclement at any moment. Well, he chuckled inwardly, if that was the way of it, good luck to her! He'd certainly no wish to spoil sport. He only hoped that the young man proved worthy of her.

The streets were deserted but for the occasional tradesman calling his wares. The only sound was the clop of horses' feet. A slight mizzle was already in the air, coating the pavements, the iron railings, and even the new green of the trees with a fine greaselike film. Its fresh earthy tang reminded

Cecily irresistibly of riding through the leafy lanes of home, and just for an instant an odd, unbidden sense of foreboding made her long to fly back to the safe, uncomplicated world of Churston. She shook the feeling off, reproached herself for what must be accounted a temporary lapse of resolution, and turned in at the park gates.

Her disappointment upon finding the park as deserted as the street was tinged with guilty relief. Perhaps, she thought hopefully, the note had been a practical joke, though no one, surely, would be so cruel? More likely she was a few minutes early.

In the far distance a lone horseman was enjoying the freedom of an uninhibited gallop down the tan, a breach of decorum that would be frowned upon later in the day. It was the only sign of life apart from the continual rustlings and cheepings above her head which intensified as mother birds chivvied their young into some kind of breakfast-time order. Cecily turned to smile at Alfred, the young groom, and a man on a horse came silently from the shelter of the trees.

Her agitation, the look of sheer panic on her face, galvanised the groom into action. But even as he moved forward, Mr Elliston said with mild contempt, 'Lady Cecily, do pray assure your groom that there is no need for stupid heroics. Had I meant you harm, I could have dropped him any time these last five minutes! I wish merely to speak with you——' he gave the man a measuring look '—out of earshot, if he would be so kind?'

If she bolted now, would he pursue her? A quick glance was sufficient to confirm her isolation. The galloping horseman had vanished from view—there was only Alfred to aid her, and though she had little doubt that he would do his utmost she had also an overwhelming conviction that Mr Elliston would not tolerate any interference. How could she risk the man's safety?

Resolved upon preserving an air of calm she was far from feeling, Cecily said reassuringly, 'P-please wait for me near the gate, Alfred. You need not be unduly concerned for me... I know Mr Elliston quite well... truly!'

As the groom obeyed, albeit reluctantly, Mr Elliston moved in alongside her, uncomfortably close, until his knee was brushing her skirt and she could see quite distinctly the way the yellow hairs in his eyebrows sprang from the pinkly pale skin. 'Very sensible,' he said. 'But then, I was sure you would be.'

She sat up very straight, looking straight ahead of her. 'You had better say what you w-wish to say quickly, for I am expecting a friend at any moment.'

He uttered a harsh laugh. 'Dolly would be flattered to hear herself thus described!' As a cold feeling gripped her, he added, 'It was a most affecting little note, was it not?'

Cecily's eyes were drawn unwillingly to his. They were calculating, faintly amused.

'You wrote it?' It was hardly even a question.

He inclined his head. 'The female mind is not difficult to fathom. I had every confidence that your curiosity would find such a lure irresistible.'

Annoyance that she had proved so predictable almost superseded her fear and dislike of his closeness. She suspected that if she attempted to urge her mount away he would follow her, so she remained quite still, enduring the odious pressure of his knee against hers, forcing herself to remain calm.

'What is it that you w-want?'

'You know what I want, Lady Cecily... what I have wanted from the first moment of seeing you...'

'Oh, but Papa said——'

He cut in. 'I know what Papa said! Unfortunately he is in no position to order things as he chooses—a fact which, with his customary irresponsibility, he has seen fit to ignore. I thus find myself obliged to approach you in this unpleasantly furtive manner.' She was aware that his eyes were flicking her over and felt herself going hot. 'How much, I wonder, do you understand?'

'I know that Papa owes you money,' she said defensively.

'Oh, he does—a lot of money!' the smooth voice agreed. 'In fact, to be painfully blunt, Lady Cecily, not only do I hold all your father's considerable gambling debts, I have also advanced him a considerable sum over and above those debts in return for a clear understanding—*a gentleman's agreement*, you might say——' there was heavy derision in the words '—that you would shortly become my wife!' He paused as though to let the full import sink in. 'Should he renege on that agreement, I would be obliged, most reluctantly, to call in the whole amount at once, together with the interest due on the principal. I need not spell out the consequences, I think? Suffice it to say that Lord Camden will be fortunate if he does not languish in the Fleet for the rest of his life, and as for the plight of his family...?'

Mr Elliston might have been discussing the weather, so unemotional was his summation, but the baldness of his words only served to heighten the very real threat implicit in their delivery. Yet to her surprise, Cecily felt suddenly calm, anger paramount rather than fear. The little toad! Did he expect her to cringe, to beg, to throw herself at his feet and cry him mercy? Never! Instinct assured her that he *had* no better nature even could she bring herself to appeal to it! But it was a desperate situation, just the same, and one which required a speedy resolution. There was only one thing she could do. Her mind was resolved for her, after all.

She was every inch an earl's daughter as she said with considerable hauteur. 'I am sorry my father misled you, sir. I am in fact on the point of becoming betrothed...and my affianced husband will be only too happy to discharge every penny of Papa's debts!' She crossed her fingers and prayed that Mr Pendle would not be so disobliging as to throw a rub in the way of her plans. 'I mean to give him leave this very night to seek an interview with Papa.' The composure with which she delivered this speech delighted her, but, even so, its effect upon Mr Elliston was nothing short of extraordinary. His pale mouth tightened. He seemed about to speak when he looked beyond her, a slow flush spreading up into his hair. Then with voice no longer smooth, he said a very rude word, swung his horse around on a tight rein and galloped away in a fury.

Puzzled, Cecily turned to see that two riders had come into the park.

'Mr Anstruther! Harry! Oh, you cannot know how pleased I am to see you both!' Taken thus by surprise, her joy was unreserved and spontaneous and most of it, Harry accepted with cheerful resignation, was not for him. This much was confirmed as she turned to Marcus to say with blushing shyness, 'It is so *good* to have you back, sir!'

'I am pleased to hear you say so, infant.'

There was an odd, ironic note in Mr Anstruther's voice which Cecily wondered at and then dismissed as Harry said in his forthright, good-natured way, 'Was that toad, Elliston, being over-familiar, Cecy?

If he was, I'll gladly go after him—pop his cork for him!'

'Oh, no!' she said quickly. 'Please! It was nothing!'

'Just as you say, m'dear.'

She was aware of Mr Anstruther looking at her keenly, but she felt quite unequal to embarking upon tedious explanations and was relieved when he said only, 'Come along home, now. You are getting wet. I can't imagine what possessed you to ride out in this way—and on such a morning.'

They turned by common consent, with the groom bringing up the rear.

'Yes, young Cecily, what did bring you out before your breakfast?' Harry chuckled. 'Some clandestine meeting, I dare say, eh? Young Pendle, was it?'

'No, indeed!' The letter crackled as she touched her pocket and she knew that she was blushing. Harry mistook the cause of her discomfiture and seemed determined to be facetious. 'The baron, perhaps? He has decided to forgive you?'

She summoned a smile. 'I don't think he w-will so soon, do you?'

Mr Anstruther said very little beyond asking after his aunt and adjuring her not to be so foolish again as to go out alone in that way.

When Portland Place was reached, Mr Anstruther lifted her down and said, still in that reserved way, that he would call later.

It was almost noon when he came. Cecily knew the instant he was in the house, though he went first to see Lady Wigmore. She had had ample time in which to compose herself, blushing as she recalled her unfeigned joy upon seeing him. Was it that, she wondered, which had caused him to behave in such an odd way? She had tried to occupy her mind by writing home, sitting at the little desk in the Chinese room beside a window that overlooked the garden. But her thoughts wandered so often into daydreams of a quite impractical nature that the letter became sadly garbled. She was obliged to tear it into shreds and begin again quite three times.

But she persevered, finding the exercise salutary to her nerves, so that by the time he came into the room and the doors were closed behind him she was able to beseech him to take a seat and ask how he had found Lady Wigmore, with every appearance of calm.

They sat opposite one another: he, looking very much as he always did, elegant, at ease—one leg crossed over the other, the tassels on his gleaming Hessians swinging gently; she, sitting very straight with her hands clasped tightly in her lap.

'Aunt Constance is very much in your debt, I think,' he said. 'She tells me that the improvement you have wrought in her condition is little short of miraculous.'

'You are pleased to tease, sir.'

'No, indeed, I am quite serious. I have seldom seen my aunt so animated! And she is not in general, as I am sure you will agree, given to exaggeration.'

Cecily protested that, in this instance, Lady Wigmore's liberation from the worst of her pain had prompted her to overstate the part her god-child had played. 'It was but a simple poultice, sir, which anyone might have applied.'

'But no one else made the least attempt to do so.' Mr Anstruther paused, fingered the riband of his quizzing glass thoughtfully. 'Perhaps you may think it churlish of me in the circumstances, Cecy, if I choose this moment to take you to task?'

Her mind was a blank. 'Have I displeased you in some way?'

'Displeased?' He appeared to consider the word, stood up, and went to stare down into the fire, one foot resting on the fender. 'Shall we say, rather, that I am disappointed?'

'But w-why? I don't understand.' She addressed the words, dry-mouthed, to the smooth broad shoulders, the pensively bent head.

'We had a kind of bargain, you and I,' he mused without looking up. 'Would you agree that I have carried out my part of it to some effect?'

'Yes, indeed. You have p-put yourself to a great deal of trouble on my behalf... I am d-deeply grateful!'

He swung around and the lazy green eyes were coolly accusing. 'Then how does it come about that I return to town after but a brief absence to find your name being bandied about at White's in connection with some fiasco in Hyde Park involving the Baron von Oppenheimer from which he seems to have emerged as a figure of fun?'

'Oh, that!' Cecily giggled with sheer relief. She explained what had happened, but he didn't appear to find it funny. She grew indignant. 'It w-wasn't my fault! You can ask Harry.' It seemed he already had. From there it was but a short step to his questioning her judgement in going out with the baron in the first place.

'I couldn't help going with him!' she spluttered. 'It w-was all perfectly proper... to have refused would have given offence, and anyway, I am very well able to decide for myself with whom I drive!' Her chin lifted, 'I can't see why you are making such a fuss just because a pompous dandy like the baron chooses to make a spectacle of himself in public.'

'I don't give a damn for the baron,' said Mr Anstruther carelessly. 'I happen to think him a loathsome little wart only fit to be laughed at. I do mind very much, however, when he is laughed at in your company!' His voice was cool. 'Offend the son and you offend the mother. The baroness may be insufferably high in the instep, but she entertains the cream of society—what she does today, the rest will do tomorrow. Until now she has reluctantly preserved the delicate balance of her relationship with Aunt Constance and you have therefore been accorded your due place at the most lavish of her assemblies. But if this gossip spreads, I doubt if even my influence will suffice to persuade her in the future to receive into her home an untutored girl, however well connected, who has succeeded in making her son a laughing-stock!'

He was taking her to task! And over something that was none of her making. 'I am not untutored! And I didn't m-make the baron a laughing-stock . . . he managed that very w-well for himself!'

'Unfortunately, the baroness won't see it that way.'

Cecily sprang up. They were quarrelling in earnest now, but though a part of her felt sick a strong sense of injustice drove her on. 'And is that all that matters to you?' she flung at him across the high back of a sofa.

'No. But it *should* matter to you! You are in no position to flout influential hostesses like the baroness.' His calmness infuriated her the more.

'Now *you* are being pompous! The baroness. I am tired of hearing about the baroness and others like her! It's all so false. I am tired of having to do and say and b-be what society expects!' Her throat was becoming constricted. 'Why should I care if a lot of silly women w-with empty lives w-want to ostracise me?'

'Perhaps you have forgotten the purpose of your visit?' He stepped closer to her so that she was obliged to look up at him. 'Or have your feelings undergone a change in other ways, too? I can't see why else you would make a secret assignation in the park with Elliston, a man you have always professed to hate. A man, moreover, who is quite unacceptable in polite circles.'

'Oh, but...' Cecily blinked rapidly. 'You cannot suppose I w-went knowingly to m-meet him?'

'What am I supposed to think? You aren't in the habit of taking early-morning rides—and there was no one else in view. Are you asking me to believe that the encounter was accidental?'

The polite disbelief in his voice distressed her far more than being obliged to admit that she had been tricked by Mr Elliston. She must explain. But she couldn't, she couldn't; she opened her mouth and nothing happened. Memories of a small girl standing tongue-tied and impotent with rage before a teasing brother rose in her mind. Oh, no! 'It...w...w...' With a frustration she hadn't known since childhood she writhed over the words that wouldn't come, drummed her clenched fists on the back of the sofa, and finally in desperation reached across it on tiptoe to grope for her reticule, where the note lay.

Mr Anstruther, appalled by the effect his criticism had wrought, went quickly to the side-table where Lady Wigmore had taken to leaving the Madeira, poured a small measure into a glass, and brought it back to Cecily, who was now struggling to open the reticule.

'Drink this,' he said gently but with quiet authority. She looked at him in gratitude and took the glass in a hand that shook so much that he retained a hold on it to guide it to her lips. 'Better?' he asked presently, regarding her bent head with concern.

Cecily nodded, still gasping a little. 'That hasn't happened for years! When I w-was small... Ben used to tease me in the horrid way that little boys do sometimes—though he was always sorry afterwards. But I w-was much worse then. I quite thought I had outgrown it.' The realisation that she had not depressed her.

Her face, which had been flushed in her distress, was now grown pale, giving her that look of vulnerability which had so appealed to him at their first meeting. He cursed his own clumsiness and drew her close, dropping a light kiss on her forehead and cradling her in his arms as though she were a child. 'Come now, infant,' he murmured encouragingly. 'Don't look so tragic! I'm sure you have outgrown it, really. The fault was all mine—I was every bit as horrid as your brother. And pompous too!' he acknowledged drolly. 'Interrogating you, attempting to order your comings and goings. Quite unforgivable, in fact!'

He peered down to see what effect his words were having. She was very still. Her face, hidden from him, was buried in the lapels of his blue superfine, but he liked the feel of her head resting against him so trustingly, the way her fair curls tumbled across his coat. He had always felt protective towards her, but now she aroused in him a tenderness unlike anything he had known before.

He would have been content for her to remain there indefinitely, but already she was begging to be released, standing back, telling him in a pink-cheeked, embarrassed way not to be idiotish, and holding out to him a paper—a letter of some kind. As he turned his mind reluctantly to its contents, Cecily explained how she had come by it.

'*That* was how Mr Elliston persuaded me to visit the park, you see,' Cecily said, adding in disgust, 'And I was so easily duped!'

'As anyone might have been,' he reassured her. 'What more natural than that you should be concerned about your father?'

'And curious about the woman who is his mistress,' she admitted.

Her frankness brought a faint smile. 'Yes, well—that, too, is natural enough. What did Elliston want?'

'To marry me.' And as his smile faded to a frown, 'Or rather, warn me of the consequences of my *not* marrying him... on account of Papa's debts. You see, Papa had rather given him cause to hope...before he saw how impossible such a union w-would be!' She hurried on as the frown deepened, and, without looking at him, said, 'But it will be all right because I have told him that he will get his money back very soon. You see,' she finished in a little rush, 'I have decided that I w-will marry Mr Pendle.'

There was an uncomfortable silence.

'I see,' he said at last, but without enthusiasm. 'And when did you come to this momentous decision?'

'This morning, as I was talking to Mr Elliston. For although Mr Pendle proposed last night, I couldn't decide then. Apart from anything else, it seemed not quite fair when he fancies himself in love with me...to...to exploit his feelings for gain!' She explained earnestly. 'He really can be so awfully gullible that he makes me feel quite old!' She sighed and said resolutely, 'But this morning I decided that I could not afford to be squeamish.'

'So Mr Pendle doesn't yet know of his good fortune?' said Mr Anstruther.

'No, b-but I mean to see Papa tonight...'

'Don't!' he said with sudden urgency. He tapped the note. 'You mustn't let this panic you. Wait at least until after Hester's ball tonight.'

The ball *he* had asked Hester to give—in order to find her a husband! A little colour ran up under Cecily's skin. 'Very well,' she agreed. 'But I don't see what difference it w-will make. I don't think I could be comfortable with a terribly grand, fashionable husband, even if one were to be p-presented to me. Besides which, Mr Pendle has asked me and no one else has! I can't help feeling that *that* must count for something!'

'But you don't care for him—you can't!' Mr Anstruther felt that he was fighting a lost cause, without being altogether sure why it should suddenly matter so much to him.

'Perhaps not.' Cecily had taken the letter from him and was engaged in putting it away in her reticule, so that her voice sounded a little muffled. 'But he has many good qualities. I d-dare say I shall grow quite fond of him in time.'

CHAPTER EIGHT

HESTER'S *bal-masqué* was destined, from the arrival of the very first carriage at her door, to be one of the most outstanding events of a glittering Season. Like most indolent people, when she made up her mind to do something, she devoted every ounce of energy to making it successful. Everyone of note had been invited, including the Prince Regent *and* the Grand Duchess of Oldenburg, sister to Czar Alexander—a potential pairing that made Sir Timothy blench when he heard it.

'It won't do, m'dear—oil and water, y'know, oil and water! Not like you to overlook a thing like that!'

Hester explained that she had had no choice. The Prince was already invited when the grand duchess had let it be known that she would be pleased to attend. 'But I have it all worked out, dearest! The Prince will not come until late—he never does. And should the grand duchess still be here, which I take leave to doubt—for she can be relied upon to find the evening so tedious that she will hardly stay above an hour—then you must take Prinny off to the Wedgwood room to play hazard until she is gone.'

The scheme seemed fraught with pitfalls to Sir Timothy, but in the end Hester was proved right. The grand duchess arrived early—fair, vivacious, and outspoken, scorning mask or domino, her only concession to fancy dress being the diamonds which weighed down her petite figure. She made scathing remarks about some of the more outrageous costumes in a harsh, overloud voice and finally called for her carriage a full half-hour before the Prince Regent was due to arrive—though the crush of vehicles in the square outside brought a confrontation uncomfortably close.

Lady Wigmore observed with a permissible degree of partiality that there wasn't a woman, young or old, who would rival Cecily that night. Hester, more than content with her own Grecian draperies, was happy to agree. Cecily's gown, fashioned by Madame Louise, was in the very palest apricot-coloured brocade. The tightly laced bodice ornamented with ruched ribbons and full skirt made her waist look tiny, while the loose pleated back accentuated her slimness, giving her added height.

Signor Franzioni had arranged her pretty hair in the semblance of a wig and with a lacy mask to complete the picture, together with a fan of lace and ivory, and a string of pearls given to her by Lady Wigmore, she looked as though she had stepped from an earlier age.

Lady Wigmore, for all her talk of remaining at home, could not in the end resist the blandishments of Sir Timothy Lambton. He prevailed upon her to travel by way of his own sedan chair—a vehicle designed for his own not inconsiderable proportions—in which she could be carried with the minimum of discomfort to her leg. She was feeling so much more the thing that when Cecily added her own entreaties the matter was settled and they were both invited to dine in Grosvenor Square before the ball.

Lady Wigmore had been looking forward to seeing Tilly von Oppenheimer's face as her godchild stole all hearts, but the baroness did not attend. A message was delivered pleading a stomach disorder—'swallowed too much of her own bile!' her old antagonist was heard to mutter—while the baron, it seemed, had been obliged to leave town in order to visit a sick friend. Cecily was sorry that his drive with her had ended in that unfortunate way, but, as Harry pointed out with indisputable logic as they went down the dance together, it was bound to happen sooner or later—*she* had been the unfortunate one to have been in his company when he made a cake of himself.

'It ain't like Marcus not to see the funny side of a caper like that! Ripped me up in fine style, though I fail to see what I could have done! Did he say anything to you?'

Cecily murmured something non-committal, not wishing to remember the events of the morning.

'Have you seen Eliza?' she asked, turning the conversation.

Harry gave a piratical leer, displaying two blackened front teeth that set her laughing. 'One could hardly miss her! I've also seen one or two of the old biddies looking askance! I'd give a monkey to know where she got hold of those Turkish harem trousers!'

'They do suit her, though, wouldn't you say?' Cecily asked innocently.

'Almost too well! I'm not sure I hold with the way she's being ogled by that Roman senator opposite. Who is he, d'you know? The face escapes me under the extraordinary mask, but the legs are vaguely familiar!'

Cecily gurgled with mirth. 'It's the Marquis of Bayldon. I believe he has decided to forsake me in favour of Eliza.'

'The devil he has!'

'She might well consider him seriously, for, as she says, she isn't getting any younger and no one else has offered for her—or, at least, no one that she cares two straws for.'

'Eliza said that?' Harry looked startled. He pushed back the fine black eye-patch which he wore in lieu of a mask, the better to read her face.

'Well, not precisely in those words, though I'm sure it was what she meant.' Cecily mentally crossed her fingers. 'And I think it is a great pity, because I have always supposed that Eliza was destined for a much more adventurous life than she is like to enjoy with the marquis.'

At this point they were separated by the dance. Cecily smiled shyly at her new partner and reflected that she had promised not to interfere, but there could be no harm, surely, in just dropping a few hints. As they came together again, Harry said, 'I wish I could see your eyes properly, young Cecily. Either you are bamming me or else——? Oh, dammit!' This last was a groan.

'It does seem an awful pity, don't you think——' she asked of him gently, and seemingly apropos of nothing in particular '—if, when most of us are obliged to settle for second and even third best, two people who are truly in love lack the necessary courage to surmount a few trifling obstacles?'

Leaving him to digest this, she looked past Harry's shoulder and saw Mr Anstruther dancing with a beautiful dark lady in a pink domino. He was in severe black and white and was quite unmistakable. He bent down to say something which must have been complimentary, for the lady laughed and floated closer, seeming to melt into his arms. The sight gave Cecily exquisite pain.

Harry, following her glance, whistled softly. 'Rosanne Devine! I say, Hester was taking a chance, inviting her, but it seems to have worked. It was she, you know...'

'I know!' Cecily said with deliberate gaiety. 'Madame Devine is the pink-rose lady. I have never considered it until now, but I suppose Mr Anstruther must be excessively wealthy to be able to command roses in that fashion in the depths of winter?'

'Excessively!' agreed Harry drily. 'But most of the matchmaking mamas have long since despaired of securing his interest. He must marry eventually, of course, though the ladies who are privileged to enjoy his favours would, on the whole, make devilish wives!'

Harry's observation reassured Cecily not at all, but it was hard to stay unhappy for long when one was young and lovely and very much in demand. When Mr Anstruther presently came in search of her, he was obliged to push his way through a crowd of admirers. He found her sipping champagne and apparently enjoying the experience enormously. Mr Pendle was at her shoulder, contriving to look like Charles I, but resembling nothing so much as a lugubrious spaniel.

Claims for Lady Cecily's hand in the *boulanger* rang on all sides, but none could match Mr Anstruther for address—his reputation was unrivalled. He took the champagne glass from her hand and extracted her amidst cries of 'shame' that were for the most part good-humoured.

'Mademoiselle,' he said with a courtly bow as they took the floor.

'Monsieur!' she sighed, curtsying deeply to express her joy. And then, 'This dance was really promised to the Duke of Blane.'

'Is he the young tulip of fashion who threatened to call me out?' He glanced down at her quizzically. 'It won't do him any harm to wait. I haven't spoken to you for all of an hour. I take it you are enjoying yourself?'

'Very much,' she insisted, buoyed up by the champagne. 'You, also, I think?' And as he seemed puzzled, 'The lady in the pink domino.'

'An old friend,' he said non-committally.

In fact, he had already taken Hester sharply to task for inviting Rosanne.

She had feigned innocence.

'But Marcus! The moment I heard she was back in Town, I was sure you would wish me to invite her!'

'Well, next time I would appreciate it if you'd ask me first!'

'Oh, dear!' exclaimed his impenitent sister, 'Have I embarrassed you? How exquisite!'

'I am never embarrassed, my dear Het. I simply prefer to run my own life.'

'But you are pleased with my poor efforts otherwise?' He lifted a laconic eyebrow. 'Dear Cecy is very popular tonight,' she rattled on. 'And I'm sure it is no wonder. She is quite the loveliest creature in the room! Only eighteen!' Hester sighed her envy.

'I have had demands for introductions from at least six gentlemen—including the Duke of Blane.'

'I've met him,' said Mr Anstruther sardonically. 'He's a bit wet behind the ears, isn't he?'

'Perhaps, but thirty thousand a year, Marcus?' she murmured. 'Does that not sufficiently compensate for his youth?'

'It might, but, mark my words, he'll probably have a couple of trustees tucked away somewhere to ensure that he don't throw himself away on someone unsuitable!'

It occurred to Hester that her brother was being overscrupulous in his efforts to find Lady Cecily a husband. It was almost as though no one was destined to meet his requirements. She began to wonder if she had not perhaps been a little hasty in putting Cecily on her guard. It would indeed be wonderful... but no, this time she would wait and see.

At midnight, supper was to be served, and this was preceded by the shedding of masks. There was a great deal of good-natured skirmishing, accompanied by squeals of mirth as several young ladies were pursued as far as the illuminated gardens by their more amorous admirers.

Cecily, determined to enjoy the evening to the full, had not gone quite so far. But she had led her pursuers a merry chase before submitting to the removal of her own mask by a slightly tipsy Mr Pendle, who had held it aloft in triumph and with quite uncharacteristic boldness had claimed a kiss.

It was a very chaste salute, but had the misfortune of being witnessed by Mr Anstruther, whose eye Cecily caught at the very moment she offered her cheek to Mr Pendle amid general laughter as her health was toasted.

Mr Anstruther didn't seem to find it half so amusing as the rest, but by now Cecily was full of bubbles like the champagne. Still hiding behind the disguise, which had had a most wonderful liberating effect upon her, she was able, without the least effort, to toss him the most blatantly provocative grin of defiance. A moment later he had moved unobtrusively to her side, removed the half-full glass from her hand, and with a murmured, 'That's quite enough of *that*!' had whisked her away to a small ante-room that led off the hall where Eliza and Harry had flopped down to regain their breath. Eliza had removed her veil and was using it to fan herself.

Cecily was dumped unceremoniously in a chair where she lay back with the unconscious grace of a kitten, wrinkling her nose at Mr Anstruther in irreverent mockery.

'What have we here?' said Harry in his best parade-ground bark. 'Are you foxed, young woman?'

She giggled. 'Certainly not! I am simply enjoying myself, or rather I was until Mr Anstruther——' she stumbled over his name '—came and spoiled sport!'

'You need some supper,' Mr Anstruther said severely, though there was a glint of amusement in his eyes. 'I don't know what Aunt Constance will say if I return her charge to her incorrigibly jug-bitten.'

'Oh, for shame!' cried Eliza, her eyes brimming with laughter. 'Take no notice of them, love! They are both sadly put out because you have not devoted your time exclusively to them.'

Amid a chorus of denials, Cecily stole a glance at Mr Anstruther and felt as if her chest were being squeezed tight. Oh, how willingly she would devote not only her time but her whole life to him! But that was only one of silly Cecy's daydreams!

Over supper Harry returned with good-natured persistence to the game of choosing suitors. 'I'll vow Lady Wigmore's door knocker won't know a moment's respite tomorrow!' He reached over to carve himself a slice from a nearby baron of beef and wagged his knife at Cecily. 'You see if I'm not right.'

When Cecily demurred, Eliza was quick to add her own generous praise.

'No, no, dear Cecy, Harry's right! You have been a success far beyond all expectation tonight. Why, I counted the Duke of Blane and Charlesworth.' She ticked them off on her fingers. 'Not to mention Monsieur Simond, Lord Widdlesham . . .'

'Oh, that was just the dress and the romantical atmosphere,' said Cecily a little uncomfortably. 'They will all feel differently tomorrow.'

'I'm not so sure about that.' Harry, more than a little disguised by this time himself, waxed lyrical. 'One or two excellent possibilities there, y'know—after all, why settle for Pendle when you might be a duchess with a little application?'

To Cecily, sipping the lemonade that Mr Anstruther had procured for her, the game had grown suddenly distasteful, as though she was about to sell herself to the highest bidder. She waited for the usual reproof from Mr Anstruther, but he said nothing. Why should he, after all? This evening had been his idea. She pushed a sliver of ham irresolutely about her plate and finally swallowed it, finding it as tasteless as parchment. 'I don't think I'd make a very good duchess,' she said, declined the syllabub with a determined smile, and stood up. 'Will you excuse me? I really should try to find Papa...h-he promised he would come this evening...I ought to have made a push to find him sooner!'

She made her way quickly out of the supper room, acknowledging several friends as she went and managing to elude Mr Pendle, who had his back towards her. It didn't strike her as incongruous that she should seek to elude the man she had resolved to marry—for nothing that had happened this evening had shifted her from that re-

simply wanted to find Papa and get the whole business over.

Outside the supper room she paused indecisively—and found Mr Anstruther beside her, his hand quite firmly taking her arm. 'This way,' he said crisply, and led her down an unfamiliar passage and into a small book-room, where soft lamplight lent a comfortable glow.

She pulled away from him as he closed the door and threaded her way between tables and chairs, her unfamiliarly full skirts catching occasionally on a jutting piece of furniture. Near the fireplace she halted and faced him.

'Don't do it, Cecy!' he said, and she didn't pretend not to know what he meant.

'I must! Don't you see? I have no wish to be discussed and exhibited like a prize specimen in the marketplace!'

'You shouldn't take any notice of Harry when he's in his cups,' said Mr Anstruther harshly. 'It isn't like that.'

'But it is! Harry is simply saying what everyone is thinking!' she cried, her throat tight. 'Oh, you have been very kind and I am vastly indebted to you, but I meant it when I said I w-wouldn't make a good duchess...to be obliged to live in this artificial way indefinitely...to have to organise grand balls like this one would *sink me*!'

'Not with the right person,' he suggested quietly, but Cecily, rushing heedlessly, scarcely registered the words.

'So I have decided that I shall do very well with Mr Pendle. He will be kind, I think...and he won't expect me to be a...sparkling hostess! And besides,' she finished in a low voice as quiet despair demolished all her fine reasoning, 'if I am to help Papa quickly, as I must, there is no other course for me to take.'

He came swiftly across the room and took her hands, holding them firmly as she tried to withdraw them. She wouldn't meet his eyes, however—her head was held high and away from him so that the lamplight accentuated the lovely delicate line of her jaw. The idea of Mr Pendle possessing her was unthinkable.

'You could marry me,' he said abruptly, surprising himself.

For a moment Cecily couldn't move—couldn't breathe, even. It was what she wanted more than anything in the world, but not this way—not for pity or expediency!

'No!' she cried with such vehemence that he was taken aback. 'Oh, how c-could you?' She snatched her hands away and began to stumble in a panic towards the door.

He was with her in a few strides, turning her to face him, seeing her lovely grey eyes swimming in tears. '*Cecy!* In God's name, what have I said that is so terrible?'

She would only shake her head. He tried to draw her close, but she resisted, murmuring thickly that she would ruin his coat.

'Damn my coat!' he said with something less than his usual éclat.

He had never thought to be caught wrong-footed this way. Every instinct in him urged caution, if he was not to send her straight into Pendle's arms.

'Will you not at least consider my offer, Cecy?' he cajoled her softly, his voice definitely persuasive. 'We deal together better than most, wouldn't you say? In fact, you have added a dimension to my life that I would be loath to relinquish. Believe me, dear infant, I would never demand of you anything that made you in any way unhappy—you could live exactly as you pleased and I can safely promise to make you a hundred times happier than you would be with Mr Pendle. As for your Papa, nothing could be simpler. I will engage to settle his affairs at once. So what do you say, Cecy? Will you do me the honour of becoming my wife?'

In the silence the ticking of a small French clock upon the mantelshelf sounded unnaturally loud.

'I cannot!' There was anguish in the stifled refusal. For a moment the temptation had been overwhelming, but almost at once she knew that it would be utterly impossible to live with him upon the terms he had set out—that to be indulged with careless affection when one wished for something quite different would be exquisite torture.

'Pray forgive me,' she whispered brokenly, and, pulling herself away from him, she ran from the room, not heeding when he called her name.

It seemed like Providence that the first person she met, almost sent flying in fact, was Mr Pendle. He straightened his wig, which their collision had knocked askew, and said with a trace of peevishness that he had been looking for her everywhere. Then he peered closer and his manner underwent a change.

'But are y-you quite w-well, dear ma'am?' he enquired solicitously. 'You seem a t-trifle distraught!'

Cecily, thus obliged to account for the lingering traces of tears, invented a tiresome speck of dirt now safely dislodged. 'Mr Pendle,' she said urgently before she could change her mind, 'I have made my decision.' She swallowed. 'If I can find Papa, I would very much like you to speak to him...'

'Oh, m-my d-dear Lady Cecily!' He clasped her hand, pressed it convulsively to his lips, so that people close by looked at first surprised and then knowing as they began to speculate upon the cause. 'So happy...so proud!' he murmured incoherently. 'Your f-father...yes, I must see your father!'

Cecily felt a hysterical desire to laugh, but, once begun, the laughter might be impossible to stop.

She took Mr Pendle firmly by the hand. 'Yes—well, perhaps Papa will be with Lady Wigmore,' she suggested. 'Shall we go and see?'

They turned and found Mr Anstruther almost in their path. Before Cecily could prevent him, Mr Pendle had launched into a garbled account of his good fortune...how it was not yet official, 'But there c-can be no objection to *your* knowing, sir!'

Throughout this peroration, Mr Anstruther looked steadily at Cecily until she was convinced she could no longer bear it, his green eyes unreadable. But the end came at last. He offered polite congratulations and, with a mocking bow, stood aside to let them pass.

'So all our efforts were for naught.' Hester, drifting to his side, watched them go. 'Cecy is to have Mr Pendle, after all!'

'So it would seem!' Her brother's pleasant voice had such a strange, clipped edge to it that she regarded him more closely. His profile was positively austere!

'Why, Marcus, I believe you really mind!'

'My dear Het,' he said in a manner that discouraged comment, 'my views on the matter are of little interest to anyone but myself. That being the case, I can see little value in airing them here.' He made her a leg and excused himself.

Hester was left with the disquieting notion that Marcus was badly rattled by Cecy's decision. He had, from his earliest days, been at his most punctilious and unapproachable when hurt. As to how far her well-meaning interference had affected Cecy's thinking, she couldn't be sure. Hester sighed. Sir Timothy had warned her that no good would come of meddling... he would be very angry if he knew!

Mr Anstruther, meanwhile, was on his way to the card-room, his sole purpose to discover, broach, and down at least one bottle of his brother-in-law's excellent port. No one watching him pass by could have guessed at the tumult raging behind that languid exterior. That he, whose reputation for sophisticated dalliance was legion, should make such a bumble broth of a simple, albeit unrehearsed, proposal of marriage was galling enough; far worse was the discovery that the recipient of his offer viewed the prospect of taking him for a husband with such repugnance that she was driven to run from him straight into the arms of that ass Pendle.

It was a crushing blow to his pride, made infinitely more painful by the suspicion even now growing in him that this slip of a girl, who had so unequivocally spurned his offer, had come to mean rather more to him that he had thought possible.

Damn Aunt Constance, he fumed with something less than fairness. It was she who had persuaded him to deviate from his oft-avowed principles—and he was richly served! But never again. Never again would he permit himself to become involved with anyone so young—or so glaringly immature!

So wrapped in his own thoughts was he that he only gradually became aware of a disturbance. As he approached the door leading to the card-room, he noticed the shocked faces, the ripple of sound fast swelling as whispers grew louder; an occasional shrill voice rose above the rest, but the disjointed words were impossible to distinguish. He was on the point of asking when Harry hailed him and came hurrying across, his handsome features uncommonly grave.

'Marcus! Thank God. Look, old fellow, where's Cecy? D'you know?' Without waiting for an answer, he blurted out, 'We've got to find her before the word gets to her. Dolly Preston is at the door in great distress, asking for her. It's Camden—damned fool's blown his brains out!'

CHAPTER NINE

MR ANSTRUTHER was admitted by Bunting at a relatively early hour on the following morning, and was informed that her ladyship wished him to go straight up to her room.

'A tragedy, sir, if I might be permitted the liberty. Quite oversetting.' The old butler's face was puckered with concern. 'We're all that fond of Lady Cecily.' He shook his head. 'Just when things was going her way, too.'

'Very true, Bunting,' Mr Anstruther agreed politely, but was disinclined to extend the conversation. It had been a long and wearisome night since that moment when he and Harry had discovered Cecily with Aunt Constance, only to find that the news had already reached them. It had been like some macabre tableau—his aunt, deeply distressed, attempting to rise from her chair; Mr Pendle, hovering ineffectually in his ludicrous costume; and Cecily—Cecily, the colour of parchment, turning instinctively to him, blank-faced with shock. As Lady Wigmore had rapped out, 'Look to her, Marcus!' he had been just in time to catch her as she slipped into oblivion.

She had come around quickly enough with the aid of a few burned feathers wafted under her nose and, apart from being numbed by the news, was soon calm and seemingly fully recovered. Hester had been all for putting her straight to bed, but she insisted upon going home. This had been accomplished with the minimum amount of fuss, and Mr Anstruther had left the two ladies in Bunting's care with a recommendation that hot drinks well laced with brandy might not go amiss.

He found his aunt out of bed and standing at the window wearing a voluminous dressing robe. She turned with relief at his entry.

'Aunt Constance, this won't do! You should be resting,' he admonished her gently, for he saw the ravages the night's events had wrought in her face.

'Rest! How can I rest with that poor child on m'mind?' But she allowed her nephew to lead her to a chair where she sank down with sudden weariness. '*Why*, Marcus? Why would he do such a crass-brained thing?'

Mr Anstruther shrugged. 'Who can tell? Intolerable pressure, perhaps. The earl's affairs were in an indescribable mess, you know.'

'But Cecy was well on her way to mending all that! She had decided to take Mr Pendle—did you know?'

'Yes, I knew,' he said evenly.

'I suppose all that will be at an end now! His kind—especially that mother of his—can be relied upon to shy away from scandal quicker than most!' Lady Wigmore thumped the arm of her chair in exasperation. 'Oh, the devil take Camden! Why couldn't he have waited?' She realised the bizarre presumption her words evoked and groaned. 'No, no—I shouldn't be so lacking in charity! I suppose there is no doubt but that it was suicide?'

'Very little,' said Mr Anstruther.

He remembered how Harry had commented in disgust, 'God! What a mess! He might have found a tidier way to put an end to his existence!' as they had viewed the remains of Lord Camden looking so tragically incongruous against the splendour of his ball dress. It seemed strange, on reflection, that he should have gone to the trouble of dressing for the ball before taking his life.

'I left Sir Timothy to do the necessary—as a magistrate he will accomplish far more than I can. There will have to be a coroner's inquest, of course, but it will be a mere formality.'

There was a soft scratching on the door and Cecily came in. She started a little upon seeing Mr Anstruther, but quickly recovered. She was wearing a plain round morning gown of lavender-grey muslin which accentuated her almost transparent pallor, but she was perfectly composed—almost too composed, he thought.

She was carrying across her arm the blue pelisse which she had worn on the day she arrived. It had been a painful process, selecting the few dresses out of so many that were suitable for mourning wear, with Lizzie sniffing noisily over the discarded ones and reminding her all the while of how she had worn this one for the breakfast at Richmond House and that one for the Seftons' ball— 'Oh, and this pretty blue, milady, that you had for your first visit to Almack's!' But milady had remained obdurate—her only concession to sentiment was the pink parasol, from which she could not bear to be parted. She addressed herself to Lady Wigmore.

'I have packed all that I am like to need, dear m-ma'am, if my portmanteau could be brought down.'

Lady Wigmore was clearly upset. 'My dear child, take what you think best, by all means, but of course you will be coming back to me.' She said it defiantly. Her eyes sought her nephew's. 'Here is this child wanting to rush away before anything is properly settled . . .'

'Well, it is understandable that Cecy should wish to be with her family—to tell them the news before they hear it elsewhere,' he said quietly.

Cecily threw him a look of gratitude. His very calmness, the unspoken sympathy, succeeded in banishing any embarrassment that might have lingered from their previous encounter. He was her familiar Mr Anstruther, in whom she might repose all her trust.

He took the pelisse from her and said gently, 'Come along. I'll have Bunting arrange for my travelling chaise to be brought around and we may go any time you choose...'

'We?' She was surprised.

'Well, you did not suppose I would let you make such a journey alone, I hope,' he said, sounding mildly aggrieved. 'But we will leave only when I have your assurance that you have eaten a proper breakfast.'

'Thank you, m'boy!' said her ladyship over Cecily's head as she enveloped her godchild in a fierce embrace. 'You have relieved me of a great worry!'

'Are there not certain...arrangements, sir?' Cecily asked of him before they left. 'I did not quite like to ask, in front of Lady Wigmore, b-but I imagine there are f-formalities...Papa's lawyer...'

'It is all taken care of, Cecy,' he reassured her. 'I have seen your father's lawyer, Mr Thornaby—and he is to come down to Churston just as soon as he has everything in hand.'

Her heart was almost too full.

Churston lay on the Gloucestershire-Oxfordshire border, a journey accomplished in a day with the aid of good horses. Cecily spent much of the first few miles sitting like a pale, still ghost until Mr Anstruther, unable to bear it any longer, said with concern, 'Would you like to talk?—or perhaps you would rather sleep. I doubt you rested much last night.'

She smiled a little wanly. 'I have no wish to be a trouble to you, but can we talk—if you wouldn't mind?' He assured her that he would not, and skilfully he began to draw her out, watching her relax gradually as she spoke about her father.

'I think what I mind most is that I was just getting to know him,' she confessed. 'At home, you see, especially in the last few years, he was never really at ease...' To say more would be to criticise her mother.

Mr Anstruther recognised her difficulty and turned the conversation to other matters. He knew that the estate was entailed upon a cousin about whom she knew very little, and he wondered what contingency plans, if any, had been made in the event of something happening to the earl. There was, it appeared, a house, not big, not part of the estate, but very pleasant and not far from the sea near Margate, where they had been used to spend the summer each year.

'Of course, we shall all be very sad to leave Churston, but it will be such a relief not to have to keep it going, and the girls have always enjoyed their visits to Margate.'

Mr Pendle's name had not been mentioned once, a curious omission, but one that Mr Anstruther was loath to rectify lest it disturb their present state of harmony by bringing back to Cecy embarrassing memories of last night. As for young Pendle—it was true that last night, as they left Hester's, he had been full of assurances that he was Lady Cecily's to command. But Lady Wigmore's view—that the mother would balk at the prospect of her son's marrying into a family that bore the stigma of suicide—was his view also. He doubted whether the boy would be strong enough to resist any pressure put upon him, and if that were to be the case then the longer Cecy remained in ignorance of it, the better. For the moment she had quite enough to contend with.

During the latter part of the journey Cecily's spirits began to flag. She talked less and less. Her lack of sleep on the previous night was beginning to tell, and the journey, in spite of Mr Anstruther's comfortable, well-sprung travelling coach, seemed unending. And yet, when they finally turned in between the massive gateposts of Churston and bumped along the meandering approach to the house between shrubberies more tangled and unkempt than she had remembered, her pleasure was tempered by the prospect awaiting her, that of breaking to her family—and to Mama in particular—the dreadful tidings about Papa.

The girls came flying from the house, almost before the wheels had stopped turning, to hurl themselves upon their travel-weary sister—Bella's eyes boldly measuring Mr Anstruther even as she hugged Cecy; Cassie, grown more beautiful than ever; and Mary, coming last like a whirlwind to throw her arms about Cecily's skirts, her face buried silently in their folds.

Pryor, their elderly butler, was smiling a welcome at the front door and in the best parlour Lady Camden, who had been dozing on a sofa before the fire, sat up with a little shriek. She hastily disentangled her arms from the fringes of her shawl in order that she might clasp her 'dearest child' to her bosom, looking, as she did so, very much like a frail, faded replica of her eldest daughter. Overcome by her emotions, she begged Cecy to explain why she had not warned them of her coming so that all might be made ready? Mr Anstruther's presence, too, set her in a flutter...she was not sure if Cook had anything prepared that was in the least suited to a gentleman's tastes...

In the middle of Lady Camden's ramblings, the governess, Miss Gilbert, who had been sitting quietly in the background with her sewing and who had seen in one unobtrusively exchanged look that all was not well with this, the senior and most favourite of her charges, rose to go and order refreshments.

But Cecily bade her wait. There was no point, after all, in withholding the bad news, though she could not bring herself to go into the details. Indeed, there was no opportunity to do so, for her mama, as she had expected, went off into a swoon and the two girls burst into tears as much from shock as anything else. By the time Lady Camden had been revived with the aid of her vinaigrette and dosed with sal volatile, she was fit for nothing but to be helped to her bed, where she lay prostrate and in tears until at last, from sheer exhaustion, she fell into a doze, still clutching her daughter's hand. Cecily, sitting there in the darkened room, was all too aware that the responsibility for them all now rested squarely upon her. Mary's unspoken need of her had been particularly moving—she had been prised from her side after repeated assurances that she was not going away again. For the present, however, she was too weary to think, and when Miss Gilbert came in to relieve her, saying quietly that her place was downstairs, she went obediently.

She was very grateful for Miss Gilbert's calming influence. It had not taken her long to discover, as she had suspected, that Miss Gilbert had in the past weeks taken upon herself duties which went far beyond those of a governess. It was one of the many things that would have to be gone into later, for Cecily doubted that adequate recompense could be made at present. But when she was married... if she was married... She sighed. That, too, must wait upon events.

Downstairs she found Mr Anstruther being entertained by the two girls, but mostly by Bella, who had not only fully recovered her spirits, but had found the time to change into her best sprigged muslin—a most unsuitable dress, in the circumstances. Bella's want of sensibility was quite mortifying to Cecily, but Mr Anstruther seemed undismayed by it. Indeed, he appeared to derive a certain amusement from Bella's determined and at times blatantly coquettish attempts to engage his interest.

He had originally expressed his intention of finding an inn nearby where he could rack up overnight, not wishing to intrude upon them at such a time. But he accepted with remarkable alacrity when Cecily had offered him a bed at Churston.

'It is not what you are used to, I know,' she said diffidently, 'but if you will not mind the room being a little shabby...'

He treated her to one of his mildly sardonic looks and said that he thought he might just manage to survive, which made her smile.

'That's better,' he said. When she supposed with unconscious wistfulness that he would be wishing to get back to London as soon as possible, he replied, 'Not in the least, Cecy, but I didn't come prepared to stay—and Aunt Constance will be anxious for news.' The sight of her white pinched face moved him to suggest that he would willingly return. There was nothing she wanted more, but, by now ashamed of her attempt to cling to him for support, she said firmly that she would not hear of any such thing.

Mr Anstruther fitted into their lives that evening with surprising ease, consuming Cook's hastily embellished dish of broiled mutton with every appearance of enjoyment and sustaining with unimpaired amiability Bella's interminable quizzing about London life, while managing to draw out the shyer Cassie. He very quickly endeared himself to Miss Gilbert, too, by taking a firm line with Cecily when she spoke of having a little something on a tray in her mother's room instead of eating properly with the rest of the family, and packing her off to bed for all the world as though she were the guest and he the one in charge.

'There is little enough of you now!' he observed in that whimsical, admonishing way that defied resistance. 'And besides, you will be of little use to your family if you wear yourself out. Have you explained to your mother yet the true nature of the earl's death?'

'Oh, no!' cried Cecily. 'She is still so... p-prostrate! And besides, you know, the more I think about it, the more I am convinced that there has been some terrible mistake made.'

He made no attempt to argue, saying simply, 'Nevertheless, I think she must be told. It will be distressing, but only think how much worse it must be if she were to hear of it from some other source—a well-meaning neighbour, perhaps. Bad news almost always travels with depressing speed.' He added gently, 'I hope you will not think me critical if I venture to suggest that your mama is nothing like so frail as she is wont to appear.'

The same unworthy thought had crossed Cecily's mind on more than one occasion, but it gave her little satisfaction now to hear it confirmed. 'You are right,' she sighed, blinking rapidly and despising the stupid weakness that kept making her want to cry. 'I m-must not shirk what is plainly my duty!'

'Oh, Cecy!' He shook his head at her.

'P-please!' she implored him, making for the stairs with almost indecent haste. 'Don't be too kind t-to me or I d-don't think I shall keep up m-my spirits!'

In bed that night, exhausted though she was, she could not resist the temptation of imagining how it would be to have Mr Anstruther there for always, to order her life. All her reasons for refusing him seemed, in her present state, unbelievably trivial. When Bella presently put her head around the door to enquire if she was awake, confiding in a conspiratorial whisper that Mr Anstruther was quite the most stylish gentleman imaginable and that if Cecy wasn't determined to marry him she was the biggest pea-goose ever and that *she* had a mind to try for him herself, Cecily buried her head in the pillow and pretended that she was asleep.

Breakfast on the following morning was a trying meal, with Cassie still in bed with a headache, Cecily and Mr Anstruther in abstracted mood, and Bella chattering away in her customary fashion. As soon as she could reasonably do so, Cecily excused herself on the pretext of going to attend her mother.

Instead she went outside, feeling a desperate need to escape from the house just for a little while, to prepare herself for the moment when Mr Anstruther would leave.

She wandered across the east lawn, seeing everywhere the air of neglect as she had never seen it before. There was a little walled garden beyond, where she had planted a new herb bed the previous year. It was clogged with weed like all the rest, and suddenly it was more than Cecily could bear. With a despairing sob, she sank down on her knees.

It was here that Mr Anstruther found her presently, still on her knees and pulling so indiscriminately at the weeds choking the plants that often both came away together.

'I came to tell you that I am ready to leave,' he said, paused and added mildly, 'Poor plants.'

Cecily drew in a sharp breath and wiped the back of her hand hastily across her eyes, disgusted as she saw what a botch she had been making of so simple a task. She stood up.

'Poor Grimshaw is g-getting too old,' she said defiantly. 'I expect he doesn't notice the w-weeds.'

'I see.' His voice was gentle. 'But it isn't your responsibility any more—or had you forgotten?'

A pause. A stifled sniff.

'Is that why you are crying?'

'I'm not crying,' she protested.

'Of course you are not,' he agreed cordially. 'How foolish of me to mistake that muddy trickle for a tear!' He took out his handkerchief and proceeded to wipe away the tears and the dirt.

She endured his ministrations stoically, but in her heart she was raging. Why, oh, why, could he not, just for once, stop treating her as if she were a child? His face was so close that for one crazy, shameless moment she was tempted to slide her fingers into the crisp hair curling at the nape of his neck, to pull his mouth down to meet hers. The force of her emotions left her shaking and ashamed—and desperately in need of some explanation for her tears. She swallowed a despairing sob and said through the constriction in her throat, 'I suddenly felt so s-sad about Papa—and so inadequate.'

'You are certainly not that.' He took her small cold hand in his, ignoring her protests that it was covered in soil, and looked at it, frowning. 'If it all gets too much, or if you have need of me, you have but to send word,' he said.

CHAPTER TEN

IF ONLY my dearest Benjamin had been spared,' declared Lady Camden in faded accents, 'we should not have lived in dread of being driven from our home at any moment by some horrid little upstart!'

Cecily, who had endured much in similar vein, expressed the hope that their cousin—the new Earl of Camden—might prove to be more understanding of their situation than her mother supposed. Her mama dismissed the sentiment as being neither here nor there... besides, she recalled Mr Merton's calling upon them once and distinctly remembered that he had been a complete nonentity.

Having survived the first excesses of grief, Lady Camden's mind was turning more and more to the vexed question of what was to become of them. She dismissed the Margate house as of no account. 'It was well enough for a holiday when you were children, though I always suspected that the timbers were prone to damp, but I cannot conceive of *living* there, my dear Cecy... my girls will never meet anyone of note in Margate!' She brightened a little. 'But then, I suppose you will be marrying Mr Anstruther quite soon... his solicitude for you is quite marked. Such a very personable young man, and eligible, too. Bella has several times read out to me little accounts of his doings from the magazines Mrs Fitzallen passes on to us.'

'Oh, but...'

'At least *you* will be settled——' she dabbed at eyes reddened by frequent bouts of weeping '—and I dare say Mr Anstruther will not care to see his wife's family thrown upon the streets!'

Cecily could not let this fiction pass. She pointed out that Mr Anstruther had accompanied her solely to oblige his aunt. She did not mention Mr Pendle, thinking it unwise to do so at this stage. There had been no communication from him and she was very much afraid that...

But in any case, Lady Camden did not wish to hear of other gentlemen. It was perfectly clear to her, she said, that Mr Anstruther held Cecy in the highest regard. His showing no immediate inclination to leave was all the proof one needed! 'I am sure that it is only a very proper delicacy of feeling for us in our trouble that has so far prevented him from declaring himself!' She sighed. 'It will have to be a quiet affair, of course...not at all what I had planned for you. If only Camden had not chosen such an inconvenient time to pass on...' It was a thoughtless remark and, for Cecily, pure agony. Mama must know the whole, and then she would see how hopeless were her aspirations.

'Mama, please! *Please* don't go on m-making plans that can never...' She clasped her hands tightly together and explained, as gently as she could, the manner of her father's demise.

Lady Camden's reaction was not at all what Cecily had expected. She sat forward, drawing her shawls about her with an unconscious grace that reminded Cecily of how she had been before her health had become an overriding obsession.

'Nonsense!' she declared in quite a spirited way. 'I cannot imagine how you came by such a story, but it is all humgudgeon, you may take my word for it!'

Her daughter felt obliged to at least make her see the possibility, but she would have none of it. Tears were sheening her eyes and her voice shook very slightly, but she remained obdurate. There had been some dreadful mistake. 'Your father would never do such a thing!'

'Oh, I am glad to hear you say so! I had not known how to tell you.'

'Oh, my poor dear Cecy!'

Suddenly and quite spontaneously their arms were about one another and they clung together, shedding a few tears. For Cecily, it was a consolation she had not looked for, and her heart was filled to overflowing with gratitude to her mama for her totally illogical, but endearing demonstration of faith—a stubborn refusal to face facts, some would call it, but at this moment Cecily didn't care.

'Dearest child, you didn't really believe such a thing of your father, I am sure!'

Cecily shook her head, but urged her mama to face facts. There would have to be an official verdict—people would talk.

'Well, I'm sure we shall know how to deal with that!' said Lady Camden.

This newfound air of resolution would have done credit to Lady Wigmore, but Cecily was clear-sighted enough to know that it wouldn't last; her mama had been for so long out of the world that she hadn't truly considered all the implications. They were only just beginning to come home to Cecily herself. With increasing pessimism she wondered if any gentleman would want her now—or her sisters? The more she considered it, the more unlikely it seemed. Oh, what a fool she had been! But for her impossible dreams of Mr Anstruther, she might now be irrevocably bound to Mr Pendle and Papa might still be alive. It was a harrowing reflection, and her guilt was made the worse by Bella's bitterness.

She, too, had taken against Margate. 'Who can we possibly meet there?' she protested. 'If we must go somewhere, let it be Bath or Brighton. Yes, Brighton,' she concluded after a moment's reflection. 'In another month or so *everyone* will be in Brighton!'

Cecily stifled her exasperation, her sensibilities already worn to shreds from her endeavours to console their mama. 'But we don't have a house *there*—and we do have one at M-margate.'

'Then let us sell the one to buy the other.'

'Oh, d-do stop being difficult!' Cecily snapped and was immediately sorry. It wasn't Bella's fault after all that her world was being turned upside down just when all might have been expected to go her way. 'Anyway,' she said, 'until Mr Thornaby arrives to tell us in w-what case Papa's affairs stand, we are in no p-position to decide anything!'

Her sister flounced across the room. 'Well, I think it most unfair! Papa did little enough for us when he was alive, and now it seems he may still blight our chances——'

'Stop it! You d-don't know what you're saying!'

Bella turned to stare at Cecily, taken aback by the note of horror in her voice.

'Papa shot himself!'

She hadn't meant to say it so baldly, but it was out now. Bella went rather white, but her shock quickly found relief in noisy tears. Appalled by her own clumsiness, Cecily ran across the room at once to comfort Bella, to tell her that nothing was certain, but her arm was angrily shrugged away. 'I think that's awful! It's the most awful thing I ever heard! It will simply ruin everything!' Bella cried, rushing to fling open the door. 'Oh, it isn't fair...if I had been the one to go to London, I would be married by now! Instead, my life is like to be ruined!' Her clasp upon the door was unintentionally melodramatic. 'And if we have to go to Margate, I shall d—' On a sob she bit back the word that had suddenly assumed a new and terrible reality. 'I shall run away!'

Bella was soon back, of course, smarting from a very real sense of grievance, but having endured a stern reprimand from Miss Gilbert, who had pointed out to her in no uncertain terms the burden that was upon Cecily at this present time. 'Gilly says we have to support you,' she said a little sulkily.

Cecily, ever ready to mend a quarrel, accepted that she had been much to blame, which roused Bella to an exasperated grin. 'I'm a selfish pig!' she declared. 'And anyone but you would tell me so!'

The reconciliation complete, the two girls went upstairs to unpack Cecily's portmanteau, which had lain untouched from the previous night. Cassie presently joined them, and as one dress after another was unfolded, there were exclamations and sighs of envy, Bella bemoaning her own plumper curves, which prevented her from trying them on. Cassie seized the pink parasol and danced dreamily around the room with it.

'Do be careful!' Cecily begged. 'It w-was a present!'

They clamoured to know more, but she would not say. She didn't want to talk about Mr Anstruther; it seemed a whole world away now—those balls and breakfasts, the drives in the park, and all the pretty dresses she had left behind...

'We must buy some black crêpe,' she said, mentally listing their resources, which were depressingly meagre. 'Perhaps we can t-take the gig into Drayton later this morning if Mama is fit to be left. We should just manage enough for one dress apiece—the rest we shall have to dye.' She hung up her favourite grey redingote in the closet with a sigh. 'I dare say if I bought some black trimming to replace the pink this would be acceptable.'

'Oh, but it looks so pretty just as it is!' wailed Cassie.

'But hardly practical, in the circumstances,' said Cecily resolutely.

The short trip into Drayton was accomplished without incident; the news, it seemed, had not travelled that far as yet. When they returned, Mrs Fitzallen was with their mother and Pryor informed Cecily that a gentleman was waiting to see her in the front parlour.

It could not be Mr Anstruther returned, or Pryor would have said—Mr Pendle, perhaps, or their lawyer, Mr Thornaby. Cecily told the girls to take the packages upstairs, loosed the strings of her bonnet, and removed it. As she straightened her hair, she noticed how the ancient pier glass, which graced the wall facing the door in the dark shabby hall, made her face look almost pallid; her plain lavender muslin dress, too, accentuated the deep-purple shadows beneath her eyes. She smoothed the creases from the dress and went with firm steps towards the parlour.

But the figure that turned from the window had neither Mr Pendle's gangling height, nor, as she quickly saw, was it their lawyer.

'Good day to you, Lady Cecily,' said the smooth-tongued Mr Elliston.

'You!' she said faintly, finding his presence in her home particularly offensive at this time. She made no attempt to set him at ease. She remained standing and he was thus forced to do the same.

'I am surprised that you should w-wish to show your face here,' Cecily brought out the words with a sureness that surprised her. 'If you have c-come hoping for any settlement of Papa's debts—I must refer you to our lawyer, Mr Thornaby, whose chambers are, I believe, in the Strand, though I think you should know—indeed I d-dare say you d-do know better than anyone—you are not like to get much s-satisfaction!'

'Satisfaction.' His bland eyes looked over her, making her feel uncomfortable. 'Now that is exactly what I have come to see you about, Lady Cecily—and to sympathise with you in your bereavement, naturally.' He wore buff breeches and an olive-green riding coat which gave his face a sallow tinge. He thrust his hands into the pockets of the latter in an attitude of arrogant complacence. 'You see, we never did finish that discussion we began in the park last week.'

Was it only last week? It seemed like a hundred years! Nervousness made her reckless. 'You m-mean the day Mr Anstruther and Major Ireland f-frightened you away?'

His jaw bunched angrily and faint colour stained the sallow skin. 'I prefer to conduct my affairs without unwarranted interference.'

'As far as I am concerned, sir, there is nothing f-further to discuss. The answer I gave you then is the one I give you now. P-Papa's death alters nothing—except perhaps that you c-can no longer use him as a threat to attempt to c-coerce me!'

For answer he smiled faintly—a smug curling of the mouth that gave her a nasty lurching feeling in the pit of her stomach.

'My dear Lady Cecily, I feel sure that you have not given your situation proper thought. Perhaps you have not yet heard from this lawyer you speak of?' He nodded. 'As I thought. Well, when you do, you will find that your family is quite destitute—and I do mean destitute.' He strolled across to within a few feet of her, looking about him in a depreciatory fashion, noting the worn seat covers, the peeling plaster work of the once-fine Adam ceiling. 'You will have to leave all this, of course—this mausoleum and its surrounding estates are entailed upon a cousin, I believe? So how do you propose to live, I wonder?'

'We do have alternative accommodations...'

'The house at Margate?' Mr Elliston shook his head regretfully. 'As I explained at our last meeting, your father's financial situation had reached point nonplus long before his death. The title and deeds of the Margate house came into my hands along with his many other gambling debts some time ago.'

Cecily felt as though a chasm had opened at her feet. In spite of her mother's objection, in spite of Bella's tantrums, the house at Margate had been her security—a home for them all if Mr Pendle cried off, as she feared he might. As a last resort, they might even have sold it in order to buy something smaller, with sufficient over to provide a small annuity which she might augment by taking up some form of employment. Without it, she had no idea where to turn.

'Do let me help you to a chair, Lady Cecily—you have turned quite alarmingly pale.'

Mr Elliston's unctuous voice invaded her disordered thoughts. His hand was on her arm, but she shook it away with considerable violence.

'Thank you,' she said through shut teeth, wishing that she didn't feel sick. 'I am perfectly all right.' He should not know how badly his disclosure had affected her. 'It is a p-pity about the house, of course, but I believe we shall not n-need it. I have other plans . . .'

He laughed softly. 'That gangling youth you sought to cozen into marriage? My dear girl, you surely don't suppose his family will permit him to damn his chance of advancement in society by embroiling himself in the kind of notoriety which attaches to a young lady whose father chooses to quit the world in such a messy and unacceptable fashion? I regret to say——' he did not sound in the least sorry '—that your Mr Pendle quit town in almost as much haste as you did yourself, urged on by his mama.'

It was no more than Cecily had expected, but the shock of actually having her fears confirmed was enough to make her reach out to grasp the back of a chair.

Her reaction was not lost on him. He added with a touch of malice, 'Nor can I hold out the least hope that any other of the fine gentlemen who might have been persuaded to offer for you will behave differently. Such a pity when your prospects seemed so bright!' He became solicitous once more. 'Are you sure you will not sit? I really think you should.'

She declined, fighting to retain her dignity.

'As you please,' he said. 'Perhaps, before you give way to despair, you might care to reconsider my proposal? We are not all so fickle, you see. I am still prepared to marry you.'

His patronising tone was an affront to her sensibilities. 'You are too k-kind, sir,' she said stiffly. 'I presume that you do n-not yourself shrink from the notoriety?'

'No. But then, I do not aspire to move in first circles. My satisfaction will derive from being able to call my wife Lady Cecily. You would want for very little and my friends, though less high-toned than you are used to, are by no means contemptible. You can hardly expect more, I think, in the circumstances. Besides——' he took her hand, ignoring her protest, and pressed it to his lips '—I wanted you from the first, my dear, and I still want you!'

Cecily snatched her hand away, rubbing it vigorously on her skirt in a way that made him look furious, and moved quickly away across the fireplace to a bellpull. But before she could grasp it, the door opened and Bella whisked in.

'Cecy? Mrs Fitzallen is about to leave and she hoped to see you... Oh!' It was an artless performance, but from the interest with which Bella eyed Mr Elliston Cecily was sure she had come in on purpose, eaten up with curiosity to see the gentleman who had been closeted so long with her sister.

'Then w-will you be so good as to go back, Bella, and tell her I shall be w-with her directly?' Cecily hoped her voice sounded reasonably normal. When Bella saw that she was not to be introduced, she gave Mr Elliston her most brilliant smile and flounced out of the room.

Annoying though Bella's intrusion had been, it had afforded Cecily the necessary time in which to marshal her thoughts. Her voice was rock-firm, though her hands shook.

'I am afraid, sir, that I c-cannot contemplate your offer now, or at any time in the future. I disliked and mistrusted you from the very first and everything you have done since has confirmed my early impressions. Furthermore, whatever the w-world says, I hold you d-directly responsible for my father's death!' A certain look in his eyes arrested her momentarily. It was gone before she could define it, but she rather thought it had been fear. 'That being so, *nothing*—and I mean nothing—will persuade me to marry you!'

Mr Elliston stood indecisively for a moment before striding to the door. There he paused long enough to look back at her, bland once more. 'I really do think you may come to regret that decision, Lady Cecily. I shall be at the George in Drayton until tomorrow, should you change your mind.'

The room was very quiet when he had left. Cecily's confidence crumbled. She sank into the chair whose back she had been clutching and succumbed to the utter hopelessness of her situation. What had all her fine defiant words achieved? Nothing. In plain terms, they had no money, no assets that she knew of, and nowhere to go. For this last, much of the blame must lie with her. She had gone to London knowing full well what was expected of her and had squandered both time and opportunity in idle pleasures and useless day-dreams. Not only had she rejected offers from two of the richest men of her acquaintance—the one out of revulsion, and that she could not bring herself to regret, the other from sheer mawkish, romantical self-indulgence—but she had chosen instead a man who had balked at the first hint of scandal! All of which seemed to display a sad want of judgement in her.

Now she must explain their plight to Mama, who still fondly imagined that Mr Anstruther was on the brink of proposing and resolving all their difficulties. If only she had been less regardful of her own feelings, less impetuous, how easily she might have gratified Mama's expectations!

A lump came into Cecily's throat as she remembered Mr Anstruther's great kindness to her over the past few days, regardless of the way she had spurned him—his insistence as he was leaving that she had but to send if she had need of him. A sob broke from her—dear God, when had she ever needed him more? She could not send for him, but might she not go to him . . . tell him . . . ask him? It was not pride which made her hesitate—where he was concerned she no longer had any pride—it was a kind of terror that he might reject her. Already in the short time since he had left, she had felt utterly bereft. But her case was desperate; if his mind had altered, then she must bear it, find some alternative solution. Perhaps Lady Wigmore would help. Quite suddenly she found herself longing for her godmother's abrasive brand of common sense.

Mr Anstruther, back in town, found the latest scandal on everyone's lips.

Lady Wigmore was scathing in her distress. 'I tell you, m'boy, there are times when I find my fellow humans little short of barbaric—makes me ashamed to be one of their number!'

'That bad, is it?'

'I have suffered visits from people who would never cross the threshold in the ordinary way, full of prurient solicitude—some like Tilly von Oppenheimer openly gloating over what she had the gall to term "my misfortune"! Well,' snorted her ladyship, 'I sent her to the right-about in no uncertain manner, but there's no denying that it's a bad business!'

'Yes. I've seen Timothy.' Mr Anstruther poured himself a glass of Madeira and sipped it thoughtfully. 'He expects the coroner to record an open verdict on Camden. It seems that a considerable amount of evidence has been brought forward by that woman he was living with, and others, to suggest that his death was not quite what it appeared.'

'You mean—not suicide?' Lady Wigmore was taken aback.

'I fear there is little hope of it ever being proved, but the degree of doubt will be sufficient in Timothy's opinion to sway the coroner's verdict.'

'Well!' said Lady Wigmore. 'It's better than nothing, I suppose—though it don't alter the fact that Cecy's chances are ruined!' Her voice softened. 'How is my little gel, Marcus? Really, I mean. You've told me all the general chitchat.'

Mr Anstruther stared pensively into his glass. 'Oh, she's—being Cecy!' He looked up, meeting his aunt's glance with a wry shrug. 'You know—putting on a brave show for the sake of her family—trying to carry the whole bunch of them, and none of them worth it in my opinion!'

'Harsh words, m'boy!'

He swung around to stare out of the window. 'The mother is an emotional limpet, the second daughter, Bella, a selfish minx who is like to cause all kinds of problems. The child Cassie is well enough, I suppose—and then there is the little one——' His voice softened slightly. 'Do you know about her?'

'Only what Cecy has told me—something of a tragic case, I gather?'

'She is—strange,' he said abruptly. 'Not a sound does she utter, and yet—oh, I don't know—one feels that she is not unintelligent. She worships Cecy! And of course there is the governess, Miss Gilbert. Now that woman is a godsend!'

Lady Wigmore was regarding his elegant back with something like comprehension. 'You seem to have assessed them all with remarkable thoroughness in the short time you were there,' she said mildly. 'Cecy won't know, of course, that her erstwhile suitor has taken fright—or rather, I suspect his mama has overridden his scruples and whisked him away to the Continent. It's good riddance as far as I'm concerned. He was never *my* choice for Cecy! But it is like to make things difficult for her, I doubt the earl has left aught but a parcel of debts—and they'll have to vacate Churston.'

'There is a house at Margate, I believe—if that hasn't gone with the rest.'

Her ladyship heaved an exaggerated sigh. 'Ah, well—it behoves us all to do what we can! I have a cottage or two at my disposal in Somerset—haven't been near 'em in years, but I dare say if the necessity arises I could have one made over to Cecy as my godchild.' She shook her head in a troubled way and sighed again. 'Though I'm bound to say I can't see Elinor taking kindly to a life of genteel poverty in a cottage!'

Mr Anstruther put down his glass and strolled across to rest his hands on the wings of his aunt's chair, leaning forward a little to look down at the old lady with a curious light in his eye. 'Dear Aunt Constance, has anyone ever told you that subtlety is not one of your more effective talents?'

She met his criticism with one of those rumbling laughs that made her chins quiver. 'Yes, m'boy, *you* have—many times.' Her mood changed abruptly so that she seemed almost to be pleading with him. 'Why don't you offer for her, Marcus?'

It was his turn to laugh—a mirthless, self-denigrating sound. 'I have already done so.'

Her optimism withered before the bitterness in his voice.

'She turned me down, ma'am—with unflattering finality.'

Lady Wigmore leaned her head back against her cushion that she might more easily see into eyes grown defensively hard. 'I don't believe it,' she said flatly.

Mr Anstruther straightened up, all expression wiped from his voice. 'But then, you are partial, I fear. The plain truth is, my dear, that I proposed to Cecily on the night of that accursed masked ball of Hester's, and was rejected with such passion, such consternation, that I might have been offering her *carte blanche*!'

Lady Wigmore grunted. 'You did make your intentions plain, I suppose? Cecy ain't precisely up to snuff when it comes to that sort of thing, y'know. Just possible she might have misunderstood?'

He flung away from her, his languid pose momentarily deserting him. 'Good God, ma'am, I'm not a callow youth! Give me credit, at least, for knowing what I am about.'

'Well, it seems to me you've made a sad botch of a simple piece of work,' said his aunt in her most forthright manner. 'Lord when I think of all y'r so-called experience of my sex—all those amorous intrigues, your undoubted facility for being able to turn a pretty compliment! Yet you can't persuade a nice little thing like Cecy to take you for a husband!'

Mr Anstruther's eyes met hers briefly. 'Incredible, is it not? Still, even you must acknowledge that my failure has its comic aspect.'

'Marcus! It ain't like you to be bitter, boy.' Lady Wigmore, unwilling to relinquish without a struggle what had become her dearest wish, made one last plea. 'Could you not ask her again? The child is fond of you, I'd swear to that.'

'As a kind of father figure, perhaps. But I fear I would find such devotion trying, if not downright inhibiting as a basis for marriage.'

'Faugh! You could very soon change that an' you are half the man I believe you to be. Is it not worth the risk?'

'I think not, ma'am.' Mr Anstruther bowed and strolled to the door, effectively discouraging further argument. 'Besides,' he drawled as a parting thrust, 'it has ever been my experience that a wise man never makes the same mistake twice.'

CHAPTER ELEVEN

MR THORNABY was a quiet, dapper little man who exuded an indefinable air of confidence and integrity. Cecily liked him on sight. In the quiet back parlour she bade him take a seat and faced him in the opposite chair, wishing very much that she looked older and more authoritative.

'I dare say you will think it a little odd in me to take you aside in this way,' she began tentatively. 'But I w-wondered, sir, if I might ask a favour of you?'

Mr Thornaby inclined his head and expressed his willingness to be of service.

'I expect you will know that Mama's constitution is of a delicate nature and I very much w-wish to spare her any unnecessary anguish. The thing is, sir, I have a p-pretty fair idea of how our affairs must stand, and while I know that your principles w-would not permit you to falsify them in any way...'

Mr Thornaby watched the delicate revealing features with interest. He had heard something of the young lady, both from Mr Anstruther and from Sir Timothy Lambton, with whom he had worked closely over this shocking business of the earl's untimely demise. He was curious now to learn what Lady Cecily would have him do.

'I wondered if you could lay them before Mama in such a way that she would not guess . . . in short, sir, if you could refrain from actually saying that Papa has left us quite without resources, I w-would be vastly obliged.'

Only Mr Thornaby's eyebrows betrayed his surprise. He put his fingers together and tapped them against his lips in a calm, judicious fashion. 'What you are suggesting, my dear young lady, is somewhat irregular.' He watched a frown form and deepen in the worried young face. He cleared his throat. 'However, I can appreciate the effect such tidings might have upon Lady Camden's sensibilities at this time.'

'Yes, that is it, exactly!' Cecily cried. 'I knew you would understand. And you will help me?'

He held up his hands still locked in an attitude of prayerful caution. 'Ah, my dear young lady! If it were that simple! My duty, you see, lies not simply in serving you or your dear lady mother. I must act as I see fit and in a manner that will benefit you all.'

'Yes, of course, I do see that,' Cecily acknowledged.

'Now, as it happens, I have not yet been able to contact the heir to your father's title and lands. He is, I believe, as are many people, travelling through France—viewing the spoils of war, as it were.' He sounded disapproving. 'But when he returns, he will quite naturally wish to take up his rightful place...'

'Which is here! Yes, I do appreciate that,' Cecily agreed again, wishing that the legal mind pursued less ponderous paths. She met his eyes and found, somewhat disconcertingly, a twinkle lurking in their sensible grey depths.

'But you would like me to come to the point,' he said drily, causing her to blush. 'Well, the point, my dear Lady Cecily, is that I can, of course, read your father's will exactly as it stands without commenting specifically upon the nature of its contents, which are unfortunately very much as you have described them.' He cocked an eye at her which conveyed without his actually saying as much that he would very much like to know how she came by such knowledge. When she declined to oblige, however, he continued with the merest shrug. 'I would, however, be failing in my duty if, by so doing, I left your family quite unprepared to face the very real possibility that they might, at a moment's notice, perhaps find themselves without so much as a roof over their heads—and no provision made to meet that eventuality. You see my difficulty?'

'Yes, of course, and indeed I am v-very grateful to you f-for your care of us, sir,' said Cecily, warming to this dry little man.

Mr Thornaby gave a little cough. 'As to that, I fear your gratitude may be somewhat premature, my dear young lady. To be distressingly frank, I find myself at a loss to know how best to advise you. But since you seem to know the gist of your father's affairs, perhaps I can explain a little further. Your father had not, I fear, much of a head for business...'

'No,' Cecily agreed readily.

He looked relieved. 'The earl, you see, made his will some time ago. In it, he appointed his brother as trustee and guardian to his children, in conjunction with your dear mother, of course.'

'But Uncle Benedict died last year.'

'Precisely. I had several times made representation to the earl that he should amend the appropriate clause, but with him it was always tomorrow!'

'Yes, I know.' Cecily remembered the times she had tried to reason with Papa only to receive good-natured put-offs.

'As a result,' sighed the lawyer, 'we now have a situation whereby you are left almost entirely without assets and without any gentleman in the family who might assume responsibility for your affairs. I am right in thinking that there is no one?'

Cecily nodded. 'This cousin?' he ventured. 'Is it at all possible that he might be persuaded to make some provision?'

'I really don't know, sir. I believe Mama has met him, but I doubt she would wish to be beholden to him.'

It was in Mr Thornaby's mind to point out that Lady Camden had very little choice in the matter, but it would be to no purpose. Instead, he cleared his throat in an embarrassed way. 'An alternative occurs to me which you may feel it presumptuous of me to mention.' She urged him to be completely honest. 'It concerns your good self, Lady Cecily,' he continued reluctantly. 'You seem, if I may be permitted to say so, to be possessed of a most delightful and practical disposition—not at all a common combination, I assure you. Yes, yes,' he insisted as Cecily confessed that she had never regarded herself in such a light, 'and it occurred to me that there must be some gentleman who would appreciate those qualities, someone in whom you could repose sufficient trust and affection, perhaps, to contemplate a union...'

'Please, Mr Thornaby, do not go on!' Cecily rushed to set him at ease. 'You are quite right... m-marriage is the obvious solution.' She told him about Mr Pendle and he tutted his distress. 'But there is someone...I hope that I may yet resolve our difficulties in the way you suggest,' she added.

blushing, 'only I need a little t-time, and that is why I wish you to spare Mama's feelings, for I am determined that whatever else may have to be sacrificed she and the girls will not suffer.'

Mr Thornaby was not at all sure that he liked this talk of sacrifice, nor was he too happy about the ill-concealed desperation with which it was uttered, but when he said that he hoped she wasn't contemplating anything of a foolish nature she was quick to reassure him. 'But I w-wonder if I might ask one more small favour of you, sir?' He lifted an eyebrow enquiringly. 'Do you m-mean to travel back to London when your business here is complete?'

He confirmed that he had booked a room for the coming night at the Stag's Head in Drayton and would be taking the nine-o'clock stage to London from there the following morning.

'Then,' Cecily was hesitant, 'do you think I c-could go with you? I have to visit m-my godmother.'

He regarded her steadily for a moment or two, and then nodded. 'Very well.'

'Oh, thank you!' Cecily sprang to her feet, and as he, too, rose, she crossed the space between them to grasp his hand. 'And could we please think of some terribly important reason why I must go to London?'

'Lady Cecily!' he said on the ghost of a laugh. 'Are you trying to make a dishonest man of me?'

She denied it vigorously. 'I take it the visit to your godmother is in some way connected with these mysterious plans of yours?'

'Yes, it is.'

'H'm. Then might I suggest perhaps...something concerning that good lady...?'

'Of course!' Cecily said with a quick grateful smile. 'Lady Wigmore's leg!'

'I beg your pardon?'

She explained about her godmother's indisposition. 'She is quite better now, of course, but I think she is about to have a relapse.' Cecily's rather tired smile changed to a mischievous grin. 'I won't ask you to tell any bouncers on my behalf, sir—if you could just endeavour to look as though you comprehend perfectly what I am about!'

This time Mr Thornaby uttered a distinct chuckle. 'I don't believe I have been party to a conspiracy since my college days! Very well, I can see that you are a sensible young lady, so you may rely upon me to play my part.' He collected up his papers and held the door open for her. 'I only hope that Lady Camden will not wish to ask me any questions of a—difficult nature.'

'If she does, then you must answer her truthfully, sir—that is clearly understood. But I think she will not.'

Cecily had judged her mother's mood well. She bore up nobly throughout Mr Thornaby's long and involved peroration, but was so visibly relieved when he came to the last of the sheaf of documents that she merely said in fading accents, 'Well! That is that!' And with a sigh, 'It is much as we had supposed. I do not mind for myself, you understand, but my poor girls!' She pressed a flimsy square of lace to her eyes. 'Are you a family man, Mr Thornaby?' He confessed that he was not. 'Then you will not appreciate my feelings at this time. Only a mother could understand!' The irrefutable logic of this left him temporarily at a loss.

'I am sure that Mr Thornaby's sentiments are everything that they should be, Mama,' said Cecily, giving him an encouraging nod.

He hastened to assure her ladyship of his sympathy and somewhat diffidently moved on to the question of the funeral; if he might know her ladyship's wishes in the matter so that arrangements could be set in hand?

Lady Camden lifted tragic eyes to his. 'My husband will naturally be interred here in the family vault. I trust we may leave the arrangements in your hands?'

He agreed and made tentative mention of the inquest, now resolved, which had of necessity delayed the normal procedures, but she was so patently uninterested in anything which touched in any way upon the reality of the situation that he did not persist.

Cecily, who was very much interested, resolved to ask him later. 'Only fancy, Mama,' she said, feeling that her moment had come. 'Mr Thornaby has brought me a most disturbing message from poor Lady Wigmore. You remember that I told you about her leg?' She expounded upon her godmother's unfortunate relapse with surprising fluency, discovering in herself a hitherto untapped capacity for storytelling, Lady Camden listened with patience rather than any real concern, the exigencies of Lady Wigmore's misfortune seeming trivial when compared with her own. She was much surprised when Cecily proposed to take advantage of Mr Thornaby's imminent return to London, to go and see for herself how Lady Wigmore did, 'For indeed she has been so very kind to me, Mama—and I do feel it is the very least I can d-do to make sure she receives the p-proper treatment, and it need not take me very long. Why I dare say I should be back almost before you have had t-time to miss me!'

It seemed a very long way to go on such an errand and at such a time, complained her mother, but if Cecy had made up her mind there was little more to be said. It was plain from her tone, however, that much more would be said, but Cecily assuaged her feelings of guilt by reminding herself that the true purpose of her visit, if realised, would be to her mother's eventual benefit.

Miss Gilbert further relieved her mind by commenting drily that Lady Camden was showing an astonishing resilience in the face of her grief. 'It's a fact,' she said, shocking her erstwhile pupil very slightly, 'that your mama has had more visitors these past few days than she would normally expect to see in a month—and it's doing her a power of good!'

Mr Thornaby was an ideal travelling companion—unobtrusive, but always there at just the right moment to secure one the least uncomfortable seat and proffer refreshments when they were most needed. He had also, in his kind, unfussy way, paid for her place on the coach, knowing full well how meagre were her funds at the present—and had brushed aside her protests with a gentle jocular promise that it should find a place in his final accounts.

Grimshaw had driven Cecily into Drayton in the gig almost before anyone else was astir. Cecily was glad it was so early as she was anxious to avoid any possibility of a confrontation with Mr Elliston. She knew that he fully expected her to have changed her mind overnight, when she realised the impossibility of her position. But he would be disappointed. For one moment, she had the most awful misgivings about how he would react when he realised she was not going to submit to his will.

Cecily had not slept well and found little chance to recoup her energies, never for long falling into more than a fitful doze throughout the journey, sandwiched as she was between a man smelling strongly of fish and a young woman with a baby that grizzled and screamed by turn, in spite of repeated efforts on Cecily's part to dissuade it. The child had, explained its mother with a shocking lack of concern, 'suffered terrible bouts of colic from the day 'e was born!'

By the time they reached London she was hot, cramped, and exhausted. Mr Thornaby tutted over her in an agreeably concerned way and demanded that a hack be summoned immediately. She was presently set down at Lady Wigmore's door with his most earnest assurances that she was not under the least obligation to him and that he looked forward with interest to hearing how she went on. He took his leave of her, saying that he would be in communication with her at Lady Wigmore's as soon as he had finalised the funeral arrangements.

As she was admitted to the house, Bunting came as close as he could remember to being jolted out of his customary air of inscrutability. To say that he beamed his pleasure would be excessive, but there was no mistaking that he was pleased to see her, for all that she looked like a pale little wraith.

'Her ladyship was surely not expecting you? She has said nothing, milady.'

Cecily drew a weary breath and began to pull off her gloves as she came down the steps and across the hall. 'N-no. Lady Wigmore d-didn't know that I was coming, Bunting. It was a s-sudden decision. Is my godmother at home?'

'I regret she is not, milady.' Bunting saw the shoulders droop a little more and was driven to reassure her. 'But she will not be long, I am sure. Mrs Longford persuaded her ladyship to attend a musical soirée at Burford House, she having been properly moped since you went away—if you will not think it presumptuous of me to make such an observation!' Cecily managed a faint smile. It was almost the longest speech she had ever heard Bunting deliver at any one time. But he was not quite finished yet. 'If you would care to step up to the Chinese room, milady, I'll arrange with Cook to provide a little light refreshment, for you must have been travelling for most of the day, and Lizzie can be airing your sheets.'

Cecily thanked him warmly, but declined the refreshments. 'Perhaps,' she said hesitantly, 'if I could just have some tea?'

In the Chinese room two lamps, one either side of the fireplace, cast soft light across the serenity of the room. She removed her bonnet and smoothed her hair with fingers that shook slightly. Instead of sitting to rest her aching bones, however, she wandered about, touching a treasure here, smoothing her hand along a bamboo back of a sofa there, leaning across the desk to admire the drooping fronds of a willow tree, its outlines silhouetted gracefully against the evening light and planted in just that position so that it could be easily seen from this window. It was good to be back! Such a few short weeks and so many memories.

Behind her the door opened. Lady Wigmore's voice, slightly puffed from climbing the stairs, exclaimed, 'Cecy, dear child! I could not believe it when Bunting told me!'

Cecily emerged from the suffocating depths of Lady Wigmore's vast bosom, dazed by her unexpectedly demonstrative welcome, and saw the slim graceful figure of Mr Anstruther outlined in the doorway.

'Cecy?' He came forward in his unhurried way to study her set face, seeing the strain in her eyes. 'Is something wrong?'

'I...' she began and could not go on.

Lady Wigmore gave her nephew a speaking look and said gruffly, 'It appears to me, child, that you are worn to a thread and will be much the better for a good night's sleep! Bunting told me you had asked for tea. You shall have it in your room.'

Cecily had not thought to have her courage tested so soon. But now that Mr Anstruther was here before her, she knew that there was no purpose to be served in putting off the moment until morning. The night would be interminable!

'If you p-please ma'am, I would be very m-much obliged if I could have a few words with Mr Anstruther.' The words tumbled out in a rush. She glanced fleetingly at his face and the rush faltered. 'I shall not keep you above a few minutes, sir.'

'I am in no hurry, Cecy,' he said quietly.

Lady Wigmore looked from one to the other, said, 'Hem! Yes, well...' murmured something about accursed pinching shoes, and went from the room, shutting the door behind her.

It was very quiet when she had gone. Mr Anstruther had ample time to observe his love. He had not seen her in mourning before—surely she had lost weight, or was it simply the slim black dress which made her look so alarmingly fragile? The lamplight cast deep shadows in the contours of her face. She bore at that moment, he thought in a sudden uprush of tenderness, an amazing resemblance to the insubstantial figures which adorned the walls.

'How may I serve you, Cecy?' he prompted her gently when she showed no immediate inclination to speak.

Now that the time had come, how did one begin? The words, rehearsed so often during the course of the journey, had become a jumble in her mind. 'You may recall, sir,' she stammered, 'a few evenings s-since... you were so obliging as to—to make me an offer... a very generous offer which I v-very churlishly refused to entertain...' Oh, it was impossible! She had not realised until this moment how impossible. She had obviously read too much into his apparent kindness, for a quick nervous glance at his face now found it wiped clean of all expression, a polite, impersonal mask...

Behind his calm exterior Mr Anstruther was quite as confused as she; he saw the agony of indecision mirrored in her eyes, watched the ribbons which fell from the high waist of her dress being slowly mangled to pieces, and all the fine protestations he had made to Aunt Constance melted away. He wasn't even curious about the cause that had driven Cecy to come to him in this way; he was just deeply thankful that she had felt able to do so. Surely it must mean that she cared? But he must go gently if he were not to shatter the brittle remnants of that pride which she wore like a shield.

'You could never be churlish, infant,' he murmured, moving nearer.

His reward was a grateful, but still-nervous glance.

'Th-thank you,' she persisted resolutely. 'But I b-beg you will be completely honest with me, for... the circumstances are vastly different from those which——'

'Enough!' Mr Anstruther had reached her side now. He rescued the ribbons from complete mutilation and possessed himself of her agitated hands. 'My dear Cecy, do not, I pray you, distress yourself any further. Let me instead assure you that my sentiments are exactly as they were—and that if you now feel able to marry me you will make me the happiest of men!'

A sigh seemed to come from deep inside her. Troubled eyes searched his face. 'You are... quite sure, sir?'

'Quite sure,' he said tenderly, and prepared to gather her into his arms in order to prove it.

But Cecily, in her relief, was resolved upon completing her piece. 'Only it seems to me that I am g-getting so much more than you. I w-will, of course, strive to—to be a good and dutiful wife——' she had lowered her eyes and so did not see his sudden frown '—but, you see, there was nothing else I could think of doing if Mama and the girls were not to be l-left completely destitute... for even if I could have found employment, which I w-well might, it simply w-would not have been enough. You see, sir, there *is* no house at Margate...'

With every stumbling word his hopes were being dashed. It was clear that she had come to him, not for love, but as a last resort.

'You don't have to explain, Cecy,' he said with infinite correctness. 'I understand perfectly.'

'How k-kind you are,' she exclaimed in stifled tones, not knowing how every word wounded him. 'But it seems m-most unfair to—to take advantage and not explain! Mr Elliston now owns the house along with everything else of Papa's that w-was not entailed—as he thought to own me, too.' There was disgust in Cecily's voice. 'And I dare say you will know that Mr Pendle has thought b-better of his offer? One cannot b-blame him, of course... the scandal...' She looked up with a return of her earlier perturbation. Mr Anstruther had gone very quiet again. He looked polite, withdrawn. 'You would say, would you not... if you also f-find the scandal distasteful?' she exclaimed anxiously.

Mr Anstruther drew a deep breath, took her by the shoulders, and propelled her towards the door. 'You are obviously very tired, infant, for you are talking a great deal of nonsense. Go to bed now and in the morning everything will seem much simpler.'

He was sitting by the window, staring pensively into the darkness, when Lady Wigmore came back into the room.

'Well!' she said. 'Cecy's all tucked up in bed with Lizzie to fuss over her and hardly a word out of her! Just fancy her turning up like that without so much as a word of warning.' When her nephew failed to venture an immediate answer, she limped across to her chair and lowered herself gingerly into it, a sure sign that she was tired, for the leg only troubled her now when she had been too long upon it. She waited hopefully until frustration made itself felt in an exasperated 'It is only my house, after all! I'm sure no one is obliged to tell me anything if they do not wish to do so!' And then, 'Lord bless us, Marcus, I shall have a fit if somebody doesn't tell me something soon!'

Mr Anstruther turned to meet her eyes and in his own there was a strangely bleak smile. 'I'm sorry,' he said. 'Did Cecy not tell you? You must wish us happy, Aunt Constance, for we are to be married.'

CHAPTER TWELVE

MR ANSTRUTHER had been right. Once the decision had been taken and was out of her hands, Cecily felt much less tense. She slept deeply and dreamlessly as she had not done in quite some time, and awoke the following morning much refreshed and, if not exactly happy, at least more philosophical about the future. She was able to visit Lady Wigmore's room in order to regale her with a full account of how matters stood at home, and accepted the old lady's drily delivered expressions of astonishment and satisfaction of her unexpected news with a reasonable degree of ease.

There was much more that Lady Wigmore could have said, but she had been warned off in no uncertain manner by her nephew, who had some idiotish notion of allowing the child to remain in ignorance of his own sentiments. Ah, well! She supposed he knew what he was about. He had experience enough—or so he thought!

It was approaching noon before Mr Anstruther arrived. He quickly dispelled the nervousness Cecily had been experiencing at the thought of seeing him by appearing exactly as he always did.

'Forgive me,' he said, lifting her hand briefly to his lips and smiling at her in that lazy way that made her heart turn over. 'I would have come sooner but there have been any number of arrangements to set in motion. Would you care to take a drive and we can decide together upon those which most affect us?'

There was, he said, no question of her rushing back home before she was fully rested, and Mr Thornaby had engaged to keep him abreast of details concerning the funeral.

'I thought you might find it easier to talk away from the house,' he said in the most amiable way possible. 'My aunt is an admirable woman and I am devoted to her, but in this instance I feel we shall do better without interruption. I don't know if you have given any thought yet as to where or, indeed, when you would like us to be married?'

Cecily blushed painfully and said that she had not.

Ideally, a prospective bridegroom might have looked for a shade more enthusiasm in his beloved, but Mr Anstruther bore his disappointment with fortitude. 'For my own part, I thought perhaps a quiet wedding in the country? Your circumstances fortunately preclude much of the nonsense which would normally arise out of a formal engagement. And also, you know, London will soon be so inundated with hordes of the populace eager for a glimpse of the czar as will make our lives a misery! I am reliably informed that the parks are to become infested with all kinds of mummery!' He shuddered. 'We shall be much better out of it!'

He might have been arranging an outing, so matter-of-fact did he sound. Cecily's heart sank. 'I shall be happy to leave the arrangements in your hands, sir,' she said, adding diffidently, 'However, I d-don't know p-precisely how long we shall be able to remain at Churston.'

'That is easily taken care of,' he assured her. 'We can be married as soon as you please. I have a property in Surrey—Holmbury—perhaps you already know of it?' She murmured that she did. It was there that he cultivated the pink roses, but she didn't add this last aloud. 'The estate is quite attractively situated in a wooded valley, and by the greatest good fortune there is a dower house occupied at present by my factor—a single man with few needs. He has been living there as much as anything to keep the building in good order, and can just as easily move elsewhere. The house would be ideal for your mother's use if she will be pleased to consider it and you will have the added satisfaction of being able to keep your family under your eye.' He glanced down at her. 'Does the idea appeal to you?'

His goodness to her was so much more than Cecily had dreamed of when first she had resolved to sink her pride and approach him, that she must be grateful. She said in stifled tones, 'You are s-so very kind, sir!'

A note of exasperation crept into Mr Anstruther's voice. 'My dear infant, if you persist in commending my kindness every time I render you some trifling service, I may eventually resort to violence!'

This brought an involuntary smile.

'Very well, you shall see,' he warned, though the muscle at the corner of his mouth quivered. 'And while I have no wish to appear carping, if you *could* stop calling me sir, I might perhaps rid myself of the tiresome notion that I am robbing the schoolroom! My name, as you are well aware, is Marcus.'

Her dimples were still in evidence as she said shyly, 'I will try to remember, s—Marcus.' How odd it seemed to address him so! Nevertheless some of her old spirit returned as she added pertly, 'But I dare say I would find it a great deal easier if *you* stopped calling me infant!'

He gave a shout of laughter. '*Touché*, sweetheart!'

Cecily was sure the endearment had slipped out without conscious thought, but she hugged it to herself with shameless indulgence.

The happy mood persisted, and when they presently heard the sound of martial music followed a few moments later by the colourful spectacle provided by the band of the Coldstream Guards marching from their barracks to Hyde Park, the giant blacks at the head striking their cymbals in a high rhythmic action, Cecily was so enthralled that she grasped Mr Anstruther's sleeve and begged him to stop so that they might watch. He was so relieved to see her pale features transformed that he reined in the curricle and suffered without the least demur the continued mangling of his coat.

Cecily's cheerfulness was such that when they at last moved on Mr Anstruther asked if she felt able to call upon his sister to give her their news. Cecily saw little point in shirking the visit, though it must of necessity bring back painful memories.

She was amply rewarded by the warmth of her reception. Sir Timothy hugged her and Hester, once over her astonishment at seeing them, rose nobly to the occasion, her quite genuine expressions of delight at the prospect of having Cecily for a sister earning her a particularly speaking glance from her brother.

'I couldn't be more pleased!' Hester declared yet again when Sir Timothy had carried Mr Anstruther off to his study. 'I only hope, dear Cecily, that you won't regard anything I might have said——' she bit her lip '—my tongue does run on sometimes! And you see how wrong one can be? I had quite underestimated Marcus's good sense!' She saw that Cecily was looking a little embarrassed, and her heavily lidded eyes widened. 'You haven't said anything to Marcus?'

'Oh, no! I wouldn't dream... that is, there was nothing *t-to* say, after all.'

'Quite so!' Hester relaxed again. 'And everything has turned out splendidly.'

When the gentlemen returned, Cecily asked Sir Timothy whether any more was known about her father's death. 'Mr Thornaby t-told me there was some talk of a doubt...'

Sir Timothy looked to Mr Anstruther, who said briefly, 'You might as well tell her.'

'There is now rather more than a doubt that your father might have been killed,' said Sir Timothy, gruffly sympathetic. 'I don't suppose the truth will ever come to light, but there is strong evidence...'

To Cecily, the idea of murder was only slightly less revolting than suicide. 'But who on earth would w-want to kill Papa? He had nothing but a mounting pile of debts.' And a daughter, she thought suddenly, a daughter who was about to become betrothed, thereby putting herself out of the reach of a certain man who... Oh, no! That was being fanciful, indeed! Yet she *had* glimpsed fear in Mr Elliston's eyes; it had not been imagination, she was sure of it. But any rational person would laugh if she attempted to accuse him on such flimsy grounds.

Mr Anstruther, mistaking her frowning concentration for distress, said briskly that they were growing far too morbid and that, in any case, Lady Wigmore would be expecting her back for luncheon.

They drove home by way of the park. There were a number of people taking the air, several of whom Cecily knew. But strangely, no one stopped to speak—some looked vaguely embarrassed, and some, when possible, deliberately veered off down an alternative path. A barouche with the unmistakable livery of the Baroness von Oppenheimer approached at a smart trot. As it passed them, she inclined her head graciously to Mr Anstruther and looked straight through Cecily as though she were not there.

At her side Cecily heard Mr Anstruther swear beneath his breath. He sent his whip whistling along the horses' flanks in the way that she had so often admired, and they increased their speed to a fast trot.

'It is because of Papa, I suppose, but I d-don't mind, you know,' she said reassuringly. 'Especially the baroness! She will consider that she has d-double cause to c-cut me on account of her son, but she is s-so disagreeable that I do not care if she never recognises me again.' When he said nothing, she added with a certain agitation. 'But that is s-selfish of me, of course. I had n-not considered your position, sir. It would be quite awful an' you were saddled with a wife who was shunned by society!'

'My dear idiotic girl! Do you imagine for one moment that society would dare presume to shun the nonpareil's bride?' There was a touch of asperity in his voice, 'Or, if it did, that I would care?'

'I'm very sorry,' she apologised, but thought that he protested too much. Was he already having regrets?

'So you should be,' he said, the crispness of his tone doing little to dispel her doubts. 'Will you be ready to go home tomorrow, do you think? I intend to acquire a special licence. We can then marry whenever we please.'

Cecily's heart, fluttering up into her throat, almost smothered her. 'Yes.'

Later that day, when she was alone in the music-room, the door opened to admit Eliza, who came in like a whirlwind fashioned of russet twilled silk. She wore a hat with an outrageous brim which shaded her eyes but quite failed to conceal their bubbling excitement, which was obviously due to more than the very real pleasure of seeing her friend so unexpectedly. Cecily emerged from the enthusiastic embrace to see Harry in the glory of his full regimentals and a smug look on his face.

'I don't even need to ask,' she exclaimed. 'Oh, I am so pleased for you both! When?'

'Tomorrow morning,' Eliza said happily. 'Harry has been declared fit and is to embark for America in two days' time. I am to go with him!'

Harry gave Cecily a meaningful grin. 'I had this sudden blinding conviction that Eliza was sorely in need of a change of scene. Are we quite mad?'

'Oh, no!' Cecily held out a hand to each of them, clasping them tightly. 'Or if you are, it is a delightful madness. I do wish you *very* happy!'

Harry looked down at her. 'Talking of happiness, we ain't the only ones, it seems, in line for congratulations.'

'Indeed, no!' exclaimed Eliza as Cecily roused herself to respond in the proper manner. 'I can't think why Marcus has been such a slow top, to come so near to losing you to Algernon Pendle! What an escape you had there, my love. I never liked him above half, but I never thought he would slink away in such a shockingly poor-spirited way—just when you most had need of support!' Eliza pressed Cecily's hand sympathetically. 'But there—it has all worked out for the best.' She glanced at Harry. 'We would like you and Marcus to be at the church tomorrow. It is to be a very simple ceremony, quite early in the morning with only immediate relatives and our very closest friends.' And with a happy sigh, 'Oh, there is so much to be done and so little time!'

The following morning was busy with leave-takings and talk of travel. Eliza and Harry were united in the quiet coolness of the church with only those they most wanted present, and, after a hastily contrived breakfast, made their adieux, full of expectations that life was going to be the most tremendous adventure.

'My only regret, my dearest friends,' Eliza confessed, embracing both Cecily and Marcus with tearful enthusiasm, 'is that we shall not be here for *your* wedding!' Harry, too, wrung Marcus's hand, kissed Cecily soundly, and wished them well, promising most faithfully to write. And then they were gone. Their obvious joy in each other's company had depressed Cecily but the bustle of their own departure afforded her little time for sadness. Lady Wigmore, who felt quite unequal to such a long journey, plied her with bracing messages for her mother, which, if delivered verbatim, would more than likely send her off into a spasm. She bemoaned the fact that she had scarcely seen her dear Cecy and here she was, off again on her travels.

'It's well enough for you youngsters!' she complained to Mr Anstruther when he arrived to take Cecily away. 'But I'm past racketing around the country in your harum-scarum fashion! Can you not arrange to be married at Holmbury, Marcus? I believe I might manage that kind of a distance.'

Mr Anstruther said he would do all that he was able, but much would depend upon Lady Camden's wishes in the matter.

Since little dependence could be placed upon Elinor Camden's state of mind, Lady Wigmore called her godchild to her before she left and put into her hands a small Chinese casket lined with purple silk in which nestled a simple but exquisite collar of amethysts with matching eardrops.

'My wedding gift to you, child,' she told the speechless girl. 'Perhaps you'll think of me sometimes when you wear 'em!'

'Oh, yes, I will!' sighed Cecily, her eyes rivalling the glowing stones. 'But I shall see you again v-very soon, shall I not?'

'So I should hope,' cackled the old lady. 'But not perhaps until after you have become Mrs. Anstruther, eh?'

Cecily blushed.

The journey home this time was accomplished in a more leisurely and considerably more stylish manner than previously. For one thing, Mr Anstruther was accompanied by his man, Trimm, who found himself in the privileged position of occupying his master's travelling chaise, together with a great quantity of baggage. Here he sat, in solitary state, clutching to his thin chest the bag containing all his most prized lotions and blackings, whose secrets were the envy of many a gentleman's valet, and contributed in no small measure to the non-pareil's being acknowledged by many as the equal of—or even, he had heard it murmured, in the way one sometimes did—superior to Mr Brummell!

The weather being clement, Mr Anstruther and Cecily travelled in the curricle, taking their time. He made light pleasant conversation, hoping to put her at her ease. She responded, diffidently at first, but with more assurance as the miles passed. Often, he found himself stealing a glance at her face when she was not aware of it, watching the changes of expression, myriad as the changes wrought by the sunlight and shadow dappling her face as they drove down sleepy, leafy lanes.

At Churston, Cecily's return, bringing Mr Anstruther, was greeted with surprise, which turned to delight upon learning their news. Explanations were scarcely heeded, which was perhaps fortunate, for Cecily rather thought they would not stand close examination. Nevertheless, she was a little surprised when Bella showed so little curiosity.

'That child has been behaving oddly for the last few days,' Miss Gilbert observed with a judicious frown. 'If I thought she'd had the least opportunity, I would say there was a young man at the back of it!'

'Good gracious! There isn't, is there?'

'Not to my knowledge. Mrs Fitzallen hasn't anyone staying with her and neither has anyone else within a reasonable distance, so far as I am aware.' She sighed. 'I suppose she is just at a funny age—neither child nor woman.'

'Poor Gilly!' Cecily exclaimed. 'We have b-been a great trial to you in recent years, haven't we? I c-can't imagine why you have stayed with us so long. You have done f-far more than you ought and often w-without adequate p-payment... No, p-please, let me say it, Gilly! I can never thank you enough for all you have done these p-past weeks, and if you think you will c-care to move to Surrey with us I shall at least be able to make you p-proper recompense.'

Miss Gilbert's sensible features turned decidedly pink. 'You had always a penchant for romantical stories with happy endings, I remember!' She blew her nose. 'Foolish child! I love you all and feel myself to be a part of the family, however small and insignificant a part, and when a family runs up against hard times everyone must do their bit. I hope,' she said sternly, 'you are not marrying Mr Anstruther solely to rescue your family from their troubles. He is a fine man—too fine to be used in that way.'

'Oh, no! That is...' Cecily blushed. 'No, I—I beg you to believe it is n-not so!' A shade of defiance crept in. 'I m-mean us to be very happy!'

Comprehension dawned upon Miss Gilbert. 'Then I am sure you will be.'

Lady Camden, of course, was not in the least surprised. 'I told you, did I not, dearest Cecy? What a good thing you decided to go down to help poor Lady Wigmore. I dare say Mr Anstruther felt a little awkward about proposing when he was here—with our bereavement so recently upon us!'

It was less than a week, Cecily thought, and already her mother had adjusted to her loss. And yet, why shouldn't she? For the little that she had seen of Papa in recent years, he had been all but dead to her for a long time. On the matter of the wedding she could not commit herself at once. Their friends, after all, were mostly around them, and, though the wedding must be a quiet one, they would surely wish to attend, to wish Cecy well! Besides, there was still no sign of their deplorable cousin.

That circumstance was to be altered dramatically not above two days after the funeral.

CHAPTER THIRTEEN

THE EARL was laid to rest in the family vault with the minimum of fuss and attended by a mere handful of mourners on a day in early June brilliant with sunshine and vibrant with new life. Mr Thornaby, ever punctilious, was present at the ceremony and spent some time afterwards closeted with Mr Anstruther, the outcome of their talk proving satisfactory to both parties. He made a point of saying how pleased he was to see his young friend again and to find her affairs so admirably settled.

Lady Camden in her widow's weeds bore the strain of the occasion with a frail fortitude which drew respectful admiration from their neighbours. 'Sarah Siddons couldn't have carried the day better,' murmured Miss Gilbert with dry irreverence, intending that only Cecily should hear her, but Mr Anstruther was standing near and gave her such a comprehending look that her embarrassment quite melted away.

'How bonny young Bella is growing,' commented Mrs Fitzallen as she prepared to leave. 'I expect she will be the next to fly the nest?'

'Don't! I beg of you, dear Mrs Fitzallen, even think of such a thing!' implored Lady Camden. 'Bella is barely sixteen, and will not, I trust, be thinking of leaving her poor mother for some time. It is enough that I must lose my dear Cecy.'

'Mama! I am only going to be p-parted from you by the expanse of the p-park, which Mr—which Marcus assures me is not above a mile.'

'I dare say. But how often will you be at home?' Lady Camden sighed. 'I cannot see so fashionable a gentleman as Mr Anstruther being content with a rustic existence. No, I must resign myself to eventual loneliness, but not quite yet. And of course,' she brightened, 'with Cecy so *well* settled, she will be able to bring the younger girls out when their time comes. I'm sure that there will be no difficulty at all in finding husbands for *them*, for you must agree, Mrs Fitzallen, they are both exceedingly promising beauties! But all that is in the future.'

Mrs Fitzallen cast Cecily a sympathetic smile and agreed. As Cecily walked with her to the door, she said with an apologetic shrug, 'My dear, I didn't mean to provoke all that! I would not have spoken had I not been so certain that I had seen Bella the day before yesterday walking down by the old spinney with a most personable young man.'

'That's odd. Miss Gilbert s-said something...' Cecily was disturbed. Bella was so headstrong. 'You are sure it was Bella? Did you know the man?'

'Well, I thought—oh, dear!' Mrs Fitzallen looked ruefully at Cecily. 'I suppose I could have been mistaken. The man was a stranger, certainly, but he looked very much a gentleman. Oh, look, my dear, forget that I ever said anything!'

Cecily couldn't forget entirely, but there were so many other things to think about. A few questions put to Cassie revealed only that Bella had been once or twice on her own recently to visit old Mrs Fogarty in the tied cottage down by the bridge. Bella accounted for her sudden philanthropy a little defensively by explaining that she had found the old lady one day down by the stream with a sprained ankle and had helped her home. It sounded reasonable enough, and Cecily resolved to dismiss it from her mind, vowing to go one day herself to visit the old lady.

'It doesn't sound like Bella,' said Mr Anstruther dismissively when Cecily told him. They were sitting on a bench in the little herb garden—now fully weeded, he noticed—where he had found her standing in rapt contemplation. 'She's a selfish little baggage—engaging, but completely self-centred and not, I would have said, given to helping old ladies! The elusive young man fits much more with the Bella I know!'

'Oh, please! Don't even think it!' Cecily pleaded. 'After all, you d-don't really know her very well, do you? Bella can b-be very kind!'

He quirked an eyebrow at her which said more than words, and, taking her hand, drew her to her feet and began to walk her back towards the house. A light warm breeze was drifting the last lingering petals from the nearby orchard to land clinging like snowflakes to the black crêpe of Cecily's dress; it teased the soft loose curls from a brow still puckered by troubled thoughts of her sister.

'Cecy?' He squeezed her hand. 'Can we forget Bella for a little while and talk about ourselves?'

She smiled nervously—apologetically.

'I really do think it is time some decision was taken about leaving Churston, which in turn raises the question of where and when our wedding is to be. Your mother is so vague about the whole business that I believe you will have to make the decision for her and present her with a *fait accompli*.'

'Oh, dear! Must I?'

Mr Anstruther looked distinctly quizzical.

'I didn't mean . . .' She began again. 'There are so many considerations. Of course I should like to be married here among all our friends, but I am n-not sure that it is practical . . . or even advisable, for with every day that Mama remains at Churston she turns her back m-more and more on the reality of the situation, so that by the t-time our cousin arrives she will resent him quite dreadfully.'

'What a wise little thing you are,' he said. 'I'm sure you are right. And there is another consideration, too. My own parents—they will naturally wish to meet you. Oh, don't worry,' he added drily as he saw her look of alarm. 'You are exactly what Mama would have chosen for me! But, apart from that, I dare say they would be hurt if they were to be excluded from the wedding celebrations, curtailed though these must be.'

'Yes, of course. I do see that,' Cecily exclaimed.

'Then I'll set it all in hand, shall I? After all, you can choose your bride clothes later at your leisure, when your period of mourning is at an end.'

Cecily stood still, hardly able to look at him as she felt her heart bumping in her throat. 'I will d-do whatever you think best, s—Marcus,' she stammered, betraying her agitation.

'Cecy, look at me!' he commanded, taking her by the shoulders. She did so. He looked uncommonly serious. 'You don't have to be afraid.'

'I'm not!'

'Then why are you trembling so?' He sounded almost angry and she could not answer. 'Good God, do you think I could ever hurt you—in any way?'

'No.'

He let his breath out on a kind of sigh. 'Well, then.' He kissed her very gently, gave her a little shake, and they resumed their walk, Cecily with her emotions in a turmoil. Near the corner of the house they saw Mary watching them in her unblinking way.

Cecily held out a hand and the child came at once to clasp it, though her eyes turned often to Mr Anstruther. Had she seen him kiss her? Cecily wondered. She had never been sure how Mary felt about Mr Anstruther, though she had never shown the fear that most strangers aroused in her.

'You know, I believe she m-must have followed you from the house.'

'Quite possibly. Mary has become my shadow! Hadn't you noticed?'

'No. How extraordinary!'

His eyebrow described a quizzical arch. Oh, why could she not think before she spoke?

'No, do not be apologising,' he said on a laugh, 'and don't change, I beg of you! Life would become that much duller if you took each word out to examine it before opening your mouth! As for Mary and myself—we have a secret, as you will see.'

Cecily felt the small hand tighten in hers as he took from his pocket a small gold timepiece, beautifully engraved and enamelled, and on a gold chain. This he unhooked and held out to Mary. To Cecily's amazement Mary relinquished her sister's hold and took the watch in both hands, painstakingly opening the case to release a tinkling cascade of melody; for the half-minute the music lasted, the little girl was totally absorbed. Then, as the final note died, she closed it just as carefully and returned it to Mr Anstruther.

There were so many things Cecily wanted to ask, but he shook his head, and so she said simply, 'Oh, how pretty! Wherever did you find it?'

'I had it made in Vienna last year. A pretty toy, is it not? Mary has become quite adept at playing it for me.' He made no further effort to engage the child's attention, but went on talking in a matter-of-fact way, scarcely appearing to notice when a small hand presently slid into his, though his lazy green eyes kindled appreciatively. Had Mr Anstruther not already taken possession of Cecily's heart, he could surely have found no better way to win her regard.

With one of her sudden changes of mood Mary left them, to run with wild abandon along the gravel drive ahead of them. Mr Anstruther watched her, a slight frown narrowing his eyes.

'Has she never made any sound?'

'No,' sighed Cecily. 'One forgets, of course, how unnerving her silence c-can be to someone new...though you have achieved so much in so short a time!'

'I wonder?' he said, still thoughtful. 'There is a man I know in Vienna—a doctor. I would like him to see Mary. We must arrange something...'

'Oh, M-Marcus!' She turned to him, hardly daring to hope. 'Do you really think we might?'

Her shining face was almost his undoing, but before he could commit himself they heard the sound of wheels crunching on the gravel. They rounded the corner of the house to find a dust-caked travelling coach drawn up at the front steps. A thin, slightly stooped man had already alighted and was endeavouring to assist a lady to descend the steps. The style and cut of her dress bespoke Paris in every line. First impressions were, however, destroyed by her voice. It was strident in tone and clearly discernible even from a distance as it complained—of the discomforts endured upon the road; of the atrocious air of neglect apparent everywhere one looked within the grounds of Churston; and last, as Pryor made a belated appearance at the head of the front steps, of the lack of so much as a menial to attend upon their arrival.

Cecily stood, mystified, staring at Mr Anstruther.

'I rather think,' he said drily, 'that your cousin is arrived!'

CHAPTER FOURTEEN

SHE pulled herself together and ran forward, hand outstretched. 'How do you do? I am Cecily Merton. You m-must forgive us, b-but we had no idea when you w-were to arrive.' She introduced Mr Anstruther, who found himself being looked over by hard bright eyes. The new earl was obviously of little account—it was the wife who would wield the power.

'We have a considerable quantity of baggage to be carried in,' she pronounced. 'I assume there *are* servants?'

'Yes—well, Pryor will see to—to that! Pray d-do let me take you inside! You m-must be exhausted, I dare say. Have you come far?'

'Only from London today.' There was a patronising note in the sharp voice. 'It is but a trifling distance when one has travelled through France and Italy over the most appalling roads!'

Cecily led the way into the front parlour, suddenly very much aware of its general air of shabbiness, the faded chintzes. She wished that it might have been the drawing-room, but that had been under covers for months now, being too large to keep warm in the winter—and anyway, they seldom had need of it.

The new Lady Camden looked about her with ill-concealed disdain as Cecily begged to be seated. 'You will t-take some refreshment? Some tea, perhaps? And I m-must see about having your rooms prepared... and inform Mama,' she added with sinking heart.

'Stop rushing about,' murmured Mr Anstruther, who had followed them in. 'I will entertain your noxious relations while you break the news to your mother.'

As she left the room, Cecily was sure she heard some reference to the proper airing of beds, which brought a martial gleam to her eye, earning her an approving smile from her fiancé.

'I do not care how soon we leave!' declared her mother two days later. 'Just so long as I do not have to endure *that woman's* pretensions for a moment longer than I must! You know that she had announced her intention of turning off all the servants, and the whole house is to be refurbished. Nothing, it seems, meets with her approval!'

Mr Anstruther said soothingly that she might take with her any of her staff that she wished to retain and the rest should be recompensed or pensioned off as she deemed appropriate.

Only Bella had at first seemed less than enthusiastic about the suddenness of their move, muttering about having to leave all her friends, but when Cecily pointed out that there would be ample opportunity to make new friends she appeared to cheer up and entered into all the plans with enthusiasm.

It was decided that they should all travel in the first place to Holmbury, and stay there until the Dower House was made over to Lady Camden's liking. For this purpose, a post chaise was engaged to supplement Mr Anstruther's own vehicles.

On the morning set for their departure everyone was astir earlier than usual. The new Lady Camden seldom put in an appearance at breakfast, and Cecily found her cousin, freed from his wife's dominating presence, inoffensively ordinary. This morning in particular he was full of embarrassed apologies lest she feel they were being driven in undue haste from their home. But with Mr Anstruther's sardonic support, she was able to reassure him.

The breakfast-room door opened abruptly in the middle of their conversation. Miss Gilbert, uncharacteristically flustered, beckoned to Cecily, who looked quickly at Mr Anstruther and went quickly from the room.

'It's Bella,' said Miss Gilbert without preamble. 'She has gone!'

'Gone? Gone where?'

'Run away—with a man! I *knew* there was someone! I have just had some garbled story from Cassie, who is in floods of tears!' Mr Anstruther came quietly from the breakfast-room as she spoke. 'As far as I could make out Bella said she had met the man here—that he is known to you.' She drew a letter from her pocket.

Cecily was seized with an awful premonition as she broke the wafer sealing the letter. It was couched in Bella's finest defiant style, full of sorrow at causing them pain, but insisting that she was very much in love, then rather spoiling her protestations by assuring Cecy that, 'Jack Elliston is very rich, as you know, so you need not be imagining that I shall go short of anything. I dare say I shall be quite as fine a married lady as you. It is what I want and I hope you will wish me happy.' She sent her best love to Mama and hoped that she would understand and forgive her.

'Oh, dear God.' Cecily sank on to the stair and put her head in her hands. 'How am I going to tell Mama?'

Mr Anstruther rescued the letter as it fluttered to the ground and read it swiftly. '*Love!* What does a scatterbrained little minx like Bella know of love?' He looked up, frowning. 'Jack Elliston?'

'He d-did come last week!'

He summoned a hovering servant and gave orders that his groom, Watt, should bring his curricle around at once. 'How long has she been gone? Does Cassie know?'

Miss Gilbert looked uncertain. 'She said at first light. Certainly Bella's bed has been slept in.'

'Two hours' start,' he said abruptly. 'I shall need luck as well as superior cattle.'

Cecily roused herself. 'You are going after them? But how will you know...?'

His tone softened. 'My dear, there is only one place Elliston can take a girl of Bella's age.'

'Gretna Green,' Miss Gilbert said quietly. 'But if he doesn't mean to marry her?'

Mr Anstruther strode to the door. 'We must hope he has at least that much decency.' He didn't sound overconfident.

'I'm coming with you.' Cecily suddenly sprang into life.

He checked and turned with a frown. 'No. You will do better here.'

'Bella will n-need me if...when you find her!' she said resolutely.

He looked grim. 'Please!' she implored him.

He looked at Miss Gilbert.

'I can do all that must be done here,' she said. 'I think Cecy is right.'

In a matter of moments Cecily had run up to her room and returned buttoning herself into her pelisse, her bonnet clutched under her arm. Mary appeared and looked from one to the other in a kind of despair. Mr Anstruther swore softly and, taking the little watch from his pocket, put it into her hand. 'Keep that safely for me until we come back.' Her hand closed on it and he saw the tension in her ease.

They spoke little on the road at first, Mr Anstruther being fully occupied with his team. Cecily had never seen the chestnuts given their heads before, and in spite of her almost unbearable worry she felt the thrill of the sheer speed. They swept through Chipping Norton without a check, to make the most of the horses' freshness.

'I wish you had told me of Elliston's visit,' Mr Anstruther said at last.

'I was n-not aware that I had not.' Cecily frowned, trying to remember. 'But it surely c-could not have made any difference?'

'Only that the Runners have been looking for him.'

Cecily stared at him. 'Why? Because of Papa? Oh, why did you not tell me that?'

He gave her a quick rueful glance. 'I didn't want you troubled. I rather suspect they were getting a little too warm and that is why he bolted.'

'But why saddle himself with Bella? Surely he would travel more swiftly alone?'

Mr Anstruther was silent for a moment as he negotiated a particularly sharp bend. Then grimly and half-reluctantly he said, 'Revenge. What better way, after all, to be revenged upon you for spurning him?'

'But that is terrible!' Cecily cried. 'I very much hope the Runners catch him and that he is punished as he deserves.'

'I very much hope that we catch up with him first,' he amended with disquieting firmness.

At Banbury Mr Anstruther was obliged to change horses. As he arranged for the stabling of his own team and Cecily consumed a glass of lemonade, one of the ostlers distinctly remembered the couple described to him. They had gone through not much above an hour since.

Mr Anstruther's eyes glinted. 'We'll have them yet!'

Cecily was beginning to find her loyalties torn; she wanted Bella back safely, but she was just beginning to realise the price she might pay. 'You won't d-do anything silly, will you?' she pleaded.

He looked at her briefly. 'I never do silly things.'

'No, but...'

They were approaching a village. At the far end of its one main street stood a small inn, set back a little—so small that Mr Anstruther paid no heed to it. As they swept past, however, Cecily exclaimed and caught at his arm. There was a light travelling chaise, half-hidden, so that they had almost missed seeing it. It had a wheel off and a man was at work, repairing it.

'It could be,' agreed Mr Anstruther softly, commending Cecily's vigilance. He reined in and turned the team with consummate skill. In the cobbled yard of the inn a coin changed hands and the man repairing the chaise proved most helpful.

'I rather think our luck is in,' said Mr Anstruther, returning to the curricle and lifting Cecily down. 'You'd better remain here and I will send Bella out to you.'

'No.' Cecily was strangely obdurate, and he frowned. 'She may need me,' she explained lamely.

He looked mildly disbelieving, but did not try to stop her.

At first glance the place seemed deserted, the landlord was nowhere to be found. But in the low-pitched coffee-room at the rear of the building they found Bella. She was huddled into one of the high-backed settles which flanked the fire, looking, in spite of all her finery, very young and frightened.

Mr Elliston stood near the window. His face, flushed to a dull red, was more expressive of his feelings than Cecily had ever seen it. His narrowed glance came finally to rest upon Mr Anstruther, yet strangely he made no move.

'The devil!' he said. 'I might have guessed *you* would turn up.'

His words were almost submerged in Bella's wail of mingled misery and relief as she flung herself into her sister's arms. 'Oh, Cecy! I was never so pleased to see anyone! Jack has been quite beastly to me and I wish I had never come!'

'He hasn't harmed you in any way?' Cecily shook her urgently.

'No, of course not!' Bella was impatient. 'But he said I was a tiresome little opportunist and he wished that he had never laid eyes on me!' She caught the hint of a sardonic smile in Mr Anstruther's eyes and turned back to her sister, her voice swelling with the force of her grievance. 'I was never more deceived, for he had no thought of marriage...he meant to *ruin* me and then abandon me...and all to spite you!' Bella's tears, owing more to self-pity than genuine grief, flowed afresh, but Cecily was so relieved to find her unharmed that she scarcely noticed.

Mr Anstruther, however, was less patient. 'Take her outside if you please, Cecy,' he said quietly. 'I will be with you directly.'

'I would rather stay,' she asserted stubbornly, suddenly horribly aware of what he intended.

'And I would be very much obliged, my dear, if you will not argue,' he said, without taking his eyes off Mr Elliston.

Panic welled up in Cecily. Bella was still clinging to her, hampering any move she might make to go to him. In her helplessness, all was forgotten but her need to make him listen, to stop him from fighting Mr Elliston as she knew he meant to do.

'Marcus!' she cried, the words torn from her. '*Please don't*...I couldn't bear it if you were—were to be killed!'

In the silence that followed he turned to see her most deeply hidden feelings laid bare; with the oddest light in his eyes he reached out a hand to her, but before he could say anything there was a discreet cough. It came from somewhere near the window.

'Begging your pardon, ma'am, but we won't have no talk of killing, if you please,' said a hoarse voice.

A man resplendent in moleskin waistcoat and low-crowned hat unfolded his long spare frame from a corner seat where he had been concealed by the high-backed settle. In one hand he held a pistol aimed in a very businesslike fashion at Mr Elliston. 'Killing is wot I don't hold with unless it's all nice and legal,' he further explained, and, turning his attention to Mr Anstruther, said apologetically, 'I'd be werry much obliged, sir, if you'd stand well out of the way of my barker.'

Mr Anstruther stepped back at once. 'Bow Street?' he hazarded.

'The werry same, sir. Pringle's the name. Been on the trail of this swell-looking cove for several days. Wanted in London, he is, where he's got a powerful lot of questions to answer concerning the demise of a certain highborn gent whose rooms he was seen leaving in werry suspicious circumstances.'

'Lord Camden?' said Mr Anstruther. 'Then I think you should know that these young ladies are the late earl's daughters.'

'Well, now—there's a thing!' The runner passed a ruminative hand across his face.

Mr Elliston had drawn in a sharp breath. 'You can't prove anything,' he insisted with something less than his usual blandness.

'Proving ain't my business,' said Mr Pringle placidly. 'Catching's my lay.'

Bella's sobs rose afresh upon finding that the man with whom she had thought to elope had been somehow concerned in the death of her father. Mr Anstruther, exasperated beyond measure, ordered her outside if she could not better contain her emotions, and Cecily, casting him a look of gentle reproach, led her sister away, secure in the knowledge that, with Mr Pringle in command of the situation, nothing terrible could happen to him.

Mr Pringle sighed his relief. 'Petticoats is werry awkward at a time like this,' he confessed. 'I have the landlord this minute engaged in securing the lock on his cellar door. He said as I could stow this cove here until I'd decided what to do about the young missy. Hadn't reckoned on him having petticoat company, d'ye see? Anyways, I'm mortal pleased you happened along when you did. Relation of yours, is she, sir?'

'She is about to become one.' Mr Anstruther sounded less than enthusiastic. 'I suppose I had better return her to her mother.' He turned, grim-faced, to Mr Elliston, who still stood intimidated by the runner's unwavering pistol, 'I am overjoyed that the law has caught up with you so promptly, Elliston. My only regret is that I have been denied the satisfaction of dealing you a sound thrashing!'

Alarm flickered in the other man's face, growing as the runner cleared his throat and said, 'Well, now, sir—it's an uncommon strange thing, but blister me if I ain't got a speck of dust in me eye. D'you know, I reckon I'd hardly notice at all if someone was to plant that cove a facer!'

When Mr Anstruther presently strode from the inn, he was flexing his knuckles in a very satisfied way. He helped the two girls up into the curricle and climbed up himself, dismissing Cecily's concern about his bruised knuckles with the brief comment that it was of little account and had, in any case, been well worth while.

Bella's spirits were already mending. Her experience had been sadly disillusioning, but she was not by nature given to repining. Her chief concern now was that she should get back into Mr Anstruther's good books as soon as possible lest her future prospects be jeopardised. To this end she took refuge in guile, allowing Cecily to pave the way for her halting apology.

Mr Anstruther found her display of humility entertaining, though he did not permit her to know it. With sardonic deliberation he treated her to a minute examination which took in every detail of her dishevelled appearance. Then he took up the reins, saying with damping severity, 'If you ever play a trick like that again, my dear Bella, I shall wring your pretty neck.'

To Cecily he said very little. She, squashed close up against him, was made miserably aware of how shamelessly she had betrayed her feelings when she had thought his life to be in danger. She studiously avoided his eyes and was grateful for Bella's non-stop chatter throughout the journey. Though even that became an embarrassment as her sister recounted in great detail how she had slipped out into the garden on that day when Mr Elliston had called so that she might make his acquaintance, how charming he had been—which Cecily found hard to believe.

'Well, it is true—and I really don't see that you can blame me, for you never told me anything about him, or how horrid he had been, so I was quite taken in!'

Cecily was relieved when they finally arrived home, for she was bitterly ashamed of her sister's behaviour. When Bella had been tearfully reunited with her mother and Miss Gilbert had been given a full account of their adventures, there was all the matter of making new arrangements for their departure to be gone into, in the midst of which she was obliged to endure much from her cousin's wife upon the subject of young people—in particular their inconsiderate ways and the lack of discipline prevailing at the present time. This drove Cecily to a vehement defence of Miss Gilbert, to which Mr Anstruther added his own appreciation of the governess's many excellent qualities.

As soon as she was able to do so unobserved, Cecily escaped, intending to go to her room. But at the foot of the staircase her hand was firmly grasped from behind.

'Oh, no! You don't escape me so easily. We have some explaining to do, you and I,' said Mr Anstruther in a strangely clipped voice.

Ignoring her protests, he led her out into the garden, striding purposefully without any of his customary languor so that she had to run to keep up with him. In the little walled garden he stopped and swung her around to face him.

'Well now,' he said pleasantly. 'Which of us is to begin?'

He had released her hand and was holding her loosely, but quite inescapably, in the circle of his arms. She plucked at the button on his coat, seeing it through a film of tears. I'm s-sorry,' she began miserably. 'I hadn't m-meant to embarrass you...' His arms were tightening and she rushed on. 'You n-needn't feel the least obligation...'

'Oh, Cecy! You little *fool*!' he exclaimed softly, and then, commanding her, 'Look at me, dearest infant!'

The way he said it this time did not make her feel in the least like a child. Hardly daring to believe the tenderness in his voice, she blinked away the tears and saw he was looking at her in a way that there could be no mistaking.

'You love me!' She said it with a sense of wonder. 'Really love me, I mean!'

'I adore you,' he murmured, his mouth on hers. His kiss removed any last lingering doubts.

'It's just like a dream,' she sighed blissfully. 'A dream I have secretly entertained since... oh, since almost the very first day...'

He held her away a little so that he could read her face. 'Then will you explain to me why, in heaven's name, you refused me when I first proposed?'

She bit her lip ruefully. 'Don't! You cannot know how bitterly I have regretted it. I was s-so sure, you see, that you could never think of me in... in *that* way——' she blushed '—and I didn't think that I could bear to be no more to you than an amusing child!'

'Oh, you ridiculous girl! Then when you came to me later? When I thought you were just using me—that you would rather have me than Elliston, you know?'

Cecily tried to pull away from him, but he would not release his hold. 'Well, I d-did need your help quite desperately, of course,' she acknowledged with that frankness he so loved. 'But by then, too, I knew that I would sooner be w-with you on any terms than have to... to live without you! I have been in love with you... oh, since the day you gave me the parasol. It seemed to me quite the most romantic thing... until I realised you had not bought it with any such motive.'

He had the grace to look ashamed. 'That was not well done of me. There was I, so intent upon presenting you to the world, exactly as I thought proper, and it never occurred to me to wonder why none of your suitors found favour in my eyes.'

Mr Anstruther's smile was full of self-mockery. 'It seems to me I have been singularly obtuse. Not only did it take me much longer to realise how dear you were to me, but I totally misread *your* feeling for me. And I thought I knew your sex! How can you love such an utter fool?'

She proceeded to show him, winding her arms shyly about his neck and offering her mouth to be kissed. He crushed her to him with an ardour that took them both a little by surprise at first, but was infinitely satisfying.

'Only think, M-Marcus,' mused Cecily on a breathless sigh, 'we might have been married for ages before either of us found out.'

He laughed softly. 'Don't you believe it, my dearest love! I doubt that either of us would have survived the first night without betraying our true feelings!'

Cecily had imagined for so long how it would be, but now that she was actually here in his arms the reality was all and more than she had hoped for.

A hand tugged imperatively at his arm. Mr Anstruther looked down to find Mary holding out to him his watch. He took it from her gravely and put it away in his pocket.

'If ever Cecy and I go away,' he promised her, 'you shall have the watch to keep until we return.'

She appeared satisfied. He picked her up and she did not resist him. Then with Mary's arm about his neck and his free arm around Cecily, they all turned back towards the house. For the second time in the space of a few days they heard the sound of carriage wheels on the drive.

'A little late in the day for visitors,' commented Mr Anstruther.

An ancient travelling coach lumbered into view, caked in a layer of dust that almost obscured the crest upon its door.

'Good grief! I know that coach—but it can't be. Aunt Constance would never attempt such a journey!'

They broke into a run and arrived at the front steps in time to hear the well-loved voice in full cry.

'Well, let the steps down, man. Haven't I endured enough? Lord, I do believe every bone in m'body has been shaken loose! Ah, Marcus, thank God for an intelligent man at last!'

'Lady Wigmore!' cried Cecily. 'Oh, I am so delighted to see you. But you must be exhausted!'

'Never mind me. You'd best get someone to attend to Picton. She's fast turning green! No stamina, that woman.'

They glimpsed a pallid face drawn back into the far corner and Cecily summoned Pryor to bring help.

Mr Anstruther set Mary down and gave Lady Wigmore his arm. 'Curiosity get the better of you, Aunt Constance?' he said, his eyes twinkling down at her.

She sniffed. 'Nothing of the kind. Bethought me it was my duty to attend the wedding.' She peered at them. 'Ain't too late, I trust?'

'No, you are just in time,' said Cecily.

'Everything is all right, is it?' beamed the old lady, taking in the two radiant faces.

'It is now,' said Cecily.

The other exciting

MASQUERADE
Historical

available this month is:

THE ARROGANT CAVALIER

Olga Daniels

The Civil War had reached Norwich, and the sacking of their shop had persuaded Master Collins and his daughter Prudence that they should join their Puritan relatives in the New World. But their journey to Harwich cost Master Collins his life, and Prudence found herself forced to trust in her rescuer, the arrogant Edward Hayward, a cavalier on the run from Cromwell's militia.

His safety became hers, but their disguise went much further than Prudence had intended!